1

Books by Jane O'Brien

The White Pine Trilogy:

The Tangled Roots of Bent Pine Lodge #1

The Dunes & Don'ts Antiques Emporium #2

The Kindred Spirit Bed & Breakfast #3

The Lighthouse Trilogy:

The 13th Lighthouse #1

The Painted Duck #2

Owl Creek #3

The Unforgettables:

Ruby and Sal #1

Maisy and Max #2

Ivy and Fox #3

Georgy and Jack #4

Emmy and Clay #5

A Christmas Novella:

Pinecones and Promises

4

Emmy

And

Clay

Connect with Jane O'Brien
www.authorjaneobrien.com
http://www.amazon.com/author/obrienjane
www.facebook.com/janeobrien.author

Contact: authorjaneobrien@gmail.com

 Cover by:
https://www.selfpubbookcovers.com/3rustedspoons

I would like to dedicate this book and the entire The Unforgettables series to my husband, Mike. He is my soundboard, my proofreader and editor, and my promoter. He has spent endless hours reading and rereading my books, as he takes notes and then dares to tread to the dark side when he offers unwanted suggestions, which I usually accept in the end. I can't imagine writing my books without him. I love him with all of my heart.

Table of Contents

There is pleasure in the pathless woods,

There is rapture in the lonely shore,

There is society where none intrudes,

By the deep sea, and music in its roar;

I love not Man the less, but Nature more.

Lord Byron

Chapter One

The flight had been fairly routine so far, except for a small amount of turbulence that had happened just as the cup was on its way to his mouth. He had managed to hang on to the hot coffee, and so had averted a crisis. He hated messy spots on his shirt or tie. He was somewhat of a neat freak. Other than that incident, everything in the first class section was quiet.

It was his first time flying in the pricey part of the plane; he decided he rather enjoyed it. The seats were spaced father apart than in coach, allowing for more leg room, which was very important for his long-legged frame. He enjoyed the plush, tufted, leather seat backs, too, and since there was no one sitting next to him or behind him, he could lower the seat all the way back and take a nap if he chose. But today the British-born American was too wired to sleep. He was on his way to London to find his mother.

What had begun as a vacation roaming the country, looking for Civil War battlefields, had turned into something altogether different. After stopping in Muskegon, Michigan to visit Lake Michigan, one of the five Great Lakes he had not yet seen, he had made a detour to the park in the center of the city. He had read in a brochure about Civil War statues that had been donated by the town's benefactor, Charles H. Hackley. While he was walking the small city park, Michael had met a fascinating woman named Ivy Marzetti, an author who wrote under the name Ivy Morton, and after talking for a bit, he had roamed into the library where he noticed a class that was being offered called "Your Biological Family and You." Michael had never been interested in looking for the woman who had given birth to him, but for some reason on that day, he made a decision to attend the class, and his life was changed forever. The class had not helped him discover any ground-breaking facts, but he had made life-long friends, and so he had decided to stay in the area. That choice had led to a purchase of a beautiful mansion on Muskegon Lake. He could afford all the best the world had to offer now, because shortly before arriving in Michigan, he had won the lottery – big time – 113 million dollars. Even after taxes he would be set for life.

Once he was settled in his new home and the research on his book had begun, he decided it was time to go to England and seriously look for her, the woman who had given him away. He wasn't sure why; it just seemed like the right thing to do. After reading a letter she had left for him, he now knew that she had been the victim of a terrible assault; she was raped by a stranger and left alone to suffer the consequences. But through strength and perseverance, she had survived and therefore so had he. But when he was born, she was still in too much of an emotional state, and couldn't bear to look at him without remembering the attack, and so she had made the sacrifice to part with her son. The letter had made it sound like she would never want to see him, but that was 26 years ago, and he was hoping things had changed. Maybe she had a family of her own now and knew the love of a child. Maybe she had regretted the decision she had made when she was a young girl. He would see what he could find, and approach her cautiously. His adoptive mother had passed away last year, and there was a void now, a hole in his heart. Perhaps this unknown woman could ease that yearning. It was all up in the air, but if nothing else, he would have a trip back to the country where he had been raised for the first thirteen years of his life. He might even look up old friends.

"Excuse me, Michael, is there anything I can get you?" asked the hostess.

He jumped at the sound of his name. Still not used to being called Michael, he smiled and answered, "No, thank you, I'm fine."

Michael Clayton Harris, III, had been called Clay his entire life. His grandfather was called Michael and his father was Mike until his grandfather passed away and then he became Michael. It was more seemly for his station in life, he said. But the little adopted child was simply called Clay, and he had been Clay until the day he introduced himself to Ivy in the park. At that time he had given her his full name, and when she called him Michael he had not corrected her. His father lived on the other side of the state, so there would be no confusion, and the timing had seemed right to take over the more adult moniker. He had had his chance to make the correction once more when he first met Jack Gaines, his now best friend along with Jack's twin brother, Rob Sutter. Jack had called him Mike; it would have been the perfect opportunity for him to mention that he was usually called Clay, but he had said nothing, and so he had become Michael to them all – all of the wonderful people he had met in the class.

It was Jack's encouragement and his fiancée's, Georgy Hart, the teacher of the class, that he should at

17

least give the search for his mother more of an effort. They said they understood if money was an issue, the flight, hotels, food, and private detective would be costly. None of his new friends knew of his big windfall. He preferred it that way so that he would not be judged or criticized in any way. They had assumed he had some money, because the house he had purchased was by far not something a poor man could afford. The upkeep and taxes alone could drain a bank account real fast. But no one ever asked questions, and they had accepted him for who he was. That's what he loved about them. So, here he was, flying across the Atlantic, with only a few clues in hand, and even fewer documents. He was both excited and nervous at the same time. How would he feel if he couldn't find her? What if he did, and she didn't want anything to do with him? Did she have another family? Does he have siblings? Grandparents? Aunts, uncles, cousins?

Before his flight took off, he had called his dad. The conversation was stilted. He seemed to be doing okay and was adjusting to being without his partner in life, but Clay and his father had never been particularly close. His brother had more in common with their father. Clay had always leaned towards his mother. He was, by far, not a mama's boy, but they had understood each other. Talk was easy. Laughter came even easier. He missed her with all of his heart. No one could ever replace her, but still ...

The plane dropped a few feet jarring Michael out of his thoughts. The pilot apologized, saying it was just some turbulence and they would be out of it soon. Heathrow was only a few minutes away, he said. Michael buckled up giving the strap an extra tug; he was almost there, and he was excited to see what was in store for him once they landed. He could feel it. Something magical was about to happen.

Chapter Two

Heathrow was very busy; he supposed it was nothing unusual. A mass of people were bumping into each other, saying 'excuse me, pardon me.' Michael had not been back to London since he was a kid; he had forgotten how polite the British can be. Since he had only brought a carry-on, he easily moved through the crowd, went out the door, and grabbed a taxi. He felt a little strange as he gave the name of his hotel, saying "The Chesterfield Mayfair, in Westminster, please." He noticed how the driver perked up, giving him extra care with his luggage. This particular posh hotel was near the

Buckingham Palace. It had a five-star rating and was luxury all the way. Just once in his life he had wanted to see what it was like to spend hundreds of dollars per night and be treated like royalty, so he had loosened the purse strings, just as he had with the first class plane seats. He was finally enjoying some of his winnings.

Michael had decided on the way over that he would make this a longer visit than he had first anticipated. What was the rush, he thought. He was no longer employed by anyone; he was a free man. He could do whatever he wished. First, though, he would follow up on a few leads and make contact with a family researcher he had found on the Internet, and then while waiting for news about his biological mother, he would visit some tourist attractions. He was especially looking forward to the National Gallery since he had always been fascinated with art. Then perhaps he would go to Trafalgar Square, Big Ben, and the Tower Bridge. He had been to all of these places when he was a kid, but so many years had passed now, that he barely remembered anything. And of course, he couldn't go back without a stop at his mother's favorite place, Selfridges and Co. He would shop in honor of her, and maybe pick up a few gifts; although there was really no one to take anything to any longer. His girlfriend had refused to move to Muskegon, so they had parted ways. Maybe his new friends in Muskegon would appreciate something from England. That was it. He would make a shopping list, and buy whatever he thought each person might like. He kept forgetting. Money was no object, now. Michael had never been one to spend money foolishly, but he thought perhaps now was the time to start indulging himself a little. He knew no one here anymore, except for a few old school friends, so he was free to try out this money thing a little without anyone looking over his shoulder.

The driver dropped him off right in front of the hotel door, eagerly helped with his luggage, and was pleasantly surprised with his rather large tip. Once he was settled in his room, Michael's stomach growled loudly, and he realized he was very hungry. He had been looking forward to his favorite food. When he lived here, he could never get enough of fish and chips. They didn't get it quite right in the States, and he was really looking forward to the fresh fish taste and light crunch he remembered. After he had splashed some water on his face and had run a comb through his hair, he was on his way again, but this time he chose to walk.

Once outside in the fresh air, Michael was rejuvenated as the explorer part of his personality took over, so he began to wander from street to street, not really caring where he was going. At one time he found himself on Clarges Street, not too far from his hotel, and when he passed a Burger and Lobster, his mouth began to water. Forgetting about the fish and chips, all he had on his mind now was the famous lobster roll. But he decided to torture himself a bit longer and walk a little more. He would stop at the restaurant on the way back, he told himself. He followed Half Moon Street to Piccadilly and then went straight to the edge of Green Park where he could see the Palace off in the distance. He turned right and continued on Piccadilly toward the Japanese Embassy, then with his rumbling stomach growing more demanding, he decided to turn back toward the restaurant. He had to weave through a few different streets, praying his sense of direction wasn't off, but soon he was rewarded with the sight of the Burger and Lobster. The place wasn't too busy so he was served immediately, and just as he had anticipated, the famous sandwich was fantastic. He never cared much for eating alone, but he had learned to deal with it in the last few months. Being a bachelor was not all that it was cracked up to be. There were no girls overtly throwing themselves at him, but when a young female gave him a certain look of invitation, he never seemed to notice. Although he was not really shy, he would never approach a woman on his own without an introduction. He knew it was old-fashioned, but it was the way he had been brought up. As he looked around at the couples laughing together, sharing a meal with the one they were comfortable with, picking off of each other's plates, he realized, sitting here by himself, that he was going to have to change his ways and be more aggressive, or he could end up a bachelor for the rest of his life.

Michael's looks were classically handsome, and his proper English upbringing showed. He carried himself in a Cary Grant sort of way, standing and sitting straight, sure of who he was, and always perfectly groomed. He was at his best in a white shirt and dark suit, but when he removed his tie and opened the collar, he could make women lose their ability to speak. Hearts would literally flutter and knees would go weak just looking into his gorgeous eyes which were fringed with long dark lashes, yet, he never seemed to notice. Michael was a one-woman man, and since he had recently separated from his long-time girlfriend, he was not really in the market for love, but if he did find someone, she would have to be special. In the meantime, he was not about to play the field; that's just not who he was. He was willing to be patient and wait until the right one came along.

At the conclusion of his meal, Michael was anxious to return to his hotel. Once his stomach was full and he was satisfied, he began to feel the effects of jet lag and had the overwhelming desire to sleep. If he didn't get up and stretch his legs, he felt he might fall asleep right at the table. Tracing his steps backwards, he found his hotel quite easily, and was rewarded with the doorman's friendly greeting and tip of the hat. Tomorrow he would contact his researcher and go over the facts he had accumulated, including the questionnaire his biological mother had left for the people who would adopt her son. He pulled it out and read it again, even though there was no need. He had memorized it the day his brother, Brad, had sent it to him. Along with a description of the newborn baby, she had listed father as unknown and then written in the words that must have been so painful for her to put down on paper -- "Please forgive me, Michael, but I was raped and could not bear to keep you." It was signed Fiona Andover.

It may not be difficult to find her, but the looming question was: would she want to see him. Was the awful event the day of his conception too traumatic for her to think about? It was over 26 years ago, but something like that could cause pain for a lifetime. He would make sure if he did find her, that he was careful with the way he approached her. It needed to be done in a tactful and respectful way. He must convey that to the researcher also, and stress that he use the utmost care. He did not intend to start off contact with his mother in a way that would send her running from him. Now that he was here, he couldn't wait. Tomorrow was a new day. A time for seeking out his parent, exploring the city of his birth and childhood, and generally doing things that tourists do. He drifted off to sleep, dreaming about what dawn might bring.

Chapter Three

Breakfast at the hotel restaurant was everything Michael had been looking forward to. He ordered a traditional fry-up, which included eggs, bangers, fried bread, grilled tomatoes, and black pudding heavy with an oatmeal filler. It was served with English breakfast tea so strong Michael swore it made his hair stand on end, so a bit of cream was required to mellow it out, but it was sure to get him through the day. He had not been allowed to drink breakfast tea when he lived here as a child. His mother said that the caffeine would stunt his growth – something he was sure she had heard in

America. But today, as an adult, he was thoroughly enjoying himself.

As soon as he felt sated and ready to start the day, Michael caught a cab to the address for the family researcher/private detective. His appointment was at nine, and he was running a bit late, but the driver promised him it was nearby, so he should be on time. The clouds were heavy and promised a typical London drizzle, if not more; being an American, he had not once thought about an umbrella. Never one to worry about a few drops of rain, he hopped out, tipped the driver, and entered the beautiful old office building. Looking like it had been built in the 18th century or earlier, it was a wonderful example of Gothic architecture with spires and turrets reaching toward the stars. The arched doorway and heavy stone construction was a shock to the senses, as it was surrounded by modern day construction of glass and steel. The entry hall was a true work of art made of rich Carrera marble and solid granite. His heels echoed on the tiled floor, sending resonant notes up to the 4th floor ceiling. Michael paused to read the names on the list next to the modern updated elevator, and once he found Blythe and Patterson, he pushed the button and waited for his ride to the third floor.

The office he was searching for was just three doors down on his left. With a quick glance at his phone to check the time, he saw that he was exactly two minutes early, but the attitude he received from the young receptionist upon entering inferred he should have arrived a little sooner. Even though he was right on time, he still had to wait outside the office door to be called and announced. Picking up his leather briefcase, he walked into the inner sanctum of Dwayne Blythe.

Mr. Blythe was quite cordial with his greeting. "Hello, Mr. Harris. So nice to finally meet you."

"And you too, Mr. Blythe."

"Please, sit down. Can I get you some tea?"

"No, thank you. I just had some breakfast tea. I'm pretty much set for the day," laughed Michael.

"Not used to our morning hair-raising beverage, are you?" chuckled Mr. Blythe. His entire face crinkled, and with his rosy complexion, white hair, and close-cut beard, he reminded Michael of Santa Claus.

"Well, you would think I could handle the caffeine – I am American, after all, but a good strong cup of morning coffee is what I'm used to."

"Ah, yes, coffee. Never acquired a taste for it. How are you enjoying your trip to London?"

"I haven't seen much so far; I plan to do some sight-seeing later today. But I'm enjoying reliving my youth in the food department."

Mr. Blythe patted his belly. "As you can see, I enjoy food a little too much. I'm afraid I've had to give up the bangers and fried bread, my favorite. Doctors' orders, you see. What do they know? I'll probably live to be one hundred like all of my relatives who never paid any attention to what they did or didn't eat."

"So true."

"So, Mr. Harris –

"Please, call me Michael."

"I'll try, but old habits are hard to break. We tend to be more formal here with our clients. Anyway, let's get down to business. I've had a chance to go over the papers you emailed me. I have good news and bad news, I'm afraid."

The color drained from Michael's face. He had not expected to hear anything of substance so soon. "Don't tell me she's dead."

"Oh, no, son. But I have found her -- "

"You found her already?"

"It wasn't really that difficult. You had her name already, and I tracked her on a birth announcement in the newspaper. When you were born they didn't protect a mothers' privacy like they do now. Each birth was posted. After that I was able to contact a brother with the same last name who lived in that area, and from there I followed the trail."

"I hope you took care in how you approached her."

"Yes, we took every precaution. We are well-known in London for being discreet. Have no fear there. So the long and short of it is, she now knows that you are looking for her."

"What did she say? Does she want to meet me?" Michael was far more invested in this than he had imagined he would be. His emotions were visible on his face, first showing excitement at the possibilities, then fear of rejection.

"I'm sorry to say that she would not commit. She has a family now. She's married and has four children and even one grandchild. She has never told anyone of the traumatic event of the day you were conceived. Even her brother thinks she was on holiday with friends for the months preceding the birth. Frankly, she's afraid of how they would view her."

"That's so disappointing. And quite a shame. She was the victim; she did nothing wrong. Is she even considering reconciling with me? Or should I just give up?"

Mr. Blythe took a deep breath. "I think it best if we wait a few months and then contact her again. She might have had a change of heart by then. She asked me specifically not to tell you how to reach her, and I have agreed to respect her wishes."

"But I'm your client, not her."

"True, but if we upset her now, I can promise you that the door will be completely closed. It's best to take it slowly and let us handle it from now on. I'll only bill you for the hours we put in. I'll wait for three or four months and try to reach out to her again. I left her my card, and if she has a change of heart, she just might contact me. One never knows."

Michael thought about his suggestion, and said, "Okay. I don't want to upset her, and I can't say I'm not surprised. I knew the situation going in." Michael stood, picked up his case, and said, "Please keep me apprised as soon as you hear something new."

"I will certainly do that. And I'm sorry, Mr. Harris – Michael. I wish I could have had better news for you. I really thought I could arrange a meeting, at least, or I wouldn't have suggested you coming all this way."

"Not a problem. At least I had a great trip, and there's still hope. Thank you for your time; I appreciate it."

"You are most welcome. I hope to call you soon."

Michael left with a heavy heart. Yes, he had been hoping to meet his mother -- that was part of it -- but the thought that her rape had been so terribly traumatic that, after all of these years, she was still not ready to talk about it, let alone about the baby she had had, was very troubling.

He rode the elevator back down alone. A single tear escaped; he was glad no one was around to see him wipe it away. As he stood in the center of the great hall, he reminded himself of the wonderful childhood he had had, and that he had been given to kind and caring parents. It was time to call his dad again. He needed to tell him what he had learned. Michael needed to hear his wisdom and strength through the phone. Feeling the urge for some fresh air, the dejected American decided to explore some more and walk off his disappointment of the morning. A nice stroll almost always perked him up.

Chapter Four

Michael exited the building to discover a traditional English drizzle. It was nothing he couldn't handle, a few drops had never stopped him from doing anything. He popped his collar up, lowered his head, and began to walk, turning first one corner and then the next. He was not the least bit worried about getting lost. There were so many black cabs passing by, that he could easily hail one when he was ready to return to his hotel.

After several minutes of walking, the tall young man began to feel better. He truly understood the predicament his mother was in, but he was also aware, now, of four half-siblings and one niece or nephew. He would love nothing better than to meet the rest of his family.

Suddenly, the rain began to fall harder, and Michael was getting wetter. Not wanting to quit walking, he decided to look for a store that might sell umbrellas, which was probably all of them. Before he had a chance to search, the heavens opened up and let loose. He had no choice but to jog into the little business across the street with the brightly colored scarves and ribbons in the window. It wasn't until he opened the door that he realized he was in some sort of mystical fortunetelling shop. There was no one in sight, so he perused the shelves which held pungent incense, fragrant candles, bangles and beads, and Taro cards. There were even crystal balls of all sizes. He picked up a miniature one thinking it would make a cute gift for Ivy since she had written about some gypsies in one of her books.

Just as he was about to bring a candle to his nose, a beaded curtain parted; the colorful glass strands clinked together making a pleasant sound like a wind chime, and sending patterns of color all over the room. When the movement stilled, a vision appeared; Michael wasn't sure if she was real at first. She was in her early twenties, and moved with the grace of a cat. A very suggestive smile played on her face, as soon as she saw Michael. In fact it seemed to be an open invitation. Her eyes ran over his whole body, top to bottom. She touched her tongue to her upper lip, which was painted as red as a ruby.

"I see you have taken refuge in my house," she said, as she swayed toward him.

He was taken aback with her boldness. She was exotic in the way she dressed, the dip of the neckline of her filmy top leaving nothing to the imagination. Petite in stature, with long dark hair, she almost looked like a child standing next to his tall frame, but he could see sexual awareness in her eyes. She was not an innocent; that much was clear.

"I'm sorry. I was caught in the rain. I was looking for someplace that might sell umbrellas."

She laughed, showing off pearly white teeth. "We are not afraid of the rain, here. You will find no umbrellas to protect you. But I could warm you up in other ways, if you like. It's not often I have a strong, handsome, American in my shop. What do you say? I can please you in the many ways I have expertise." She was so close now, that she was brushing one breast against his arm.

Michael took a step back. He had not come to London to find a prostitute. "No, thank you. I just wanted an umbrella, but since you don't have one, I'll take this crystal ball, please."

She pouted a bit, and then smiled again. "But perhaps you misunderstood. I am not for sale. I only thought to give you comfort until the storm passed."

"Oh, I see," replied Michael. "I'm sorry if I insulted you. It's just that –

She tugged at his arm. "Don't worry. It's forgiven. Come with me. I will tell you things you have a need to know, and maybe then you will change your mind about me."

"Oh, um, okay." Michael cleared his throat. His heart was pounding; he had no idea why. He was not afraid of women -- he was single, and the two of them were alone. What would it matter to anyone if he went with her? But it's not who he was, and it could be a trap. Maybe after they had completed their, uh, business, he would be robbed and, worse yet, beat up. "Uh, better yet. No thank you. I'll just take my purchase, please."

She smiled sweetly. "You are a man of much integrity. I can see that now, without any help from the crystals. If you will allow me, I would like to do a reading for you. I have much to say."

He had time to kill until the rain let up. The reading might be good for a laugh, and he would have a nice story to tell when he returned to the States. "Okay, but that's it. I have to be somewhere. I don't have much time."

"I do not think that is true, so come sit with me. Here, across the table. I will only touch your hands, I promise."

She took his hand, pulling him into the room beyond the curtain. It was everything a person would think a fortunetelling setup would be – burning candles, a crystal ball, some peacock feathers, oddly enough, and a tall golden goblet on a side table. On the back wall, Michael noticed an ancient map, yellowed in color and torn around the edges. He could not read the words because they were in some sort of Cyrillic script. It might be Polish or Russian, but it was most definitely an Eastern European country, Slavic perhaps. He thought by the placement of other countries around its borders, it might be Ukraine, if he remembered his geography correctly.

The woman seated herself and gestured for him to do the same. She stretched out her arm to clasp his hands in hers. Her fingers were decorated with rings of many colored gemstones, but what caught his eye was a beautiful sapphire and diamond bracelet on her wrist. It flashed in the low light, and sent small electrical sparks that arced from her arm to his. He did not get an electrical shock, but it surprised him, causing him to jump. She gently pulled him back. "You see? We were meant to talk. I knew it the moment you came in. This has never happened before."

"What do you mean?"

"Will you trust me, Michael, or should I call you Clay?"

"What? How did you know to call me that? How do you know my name? No one calls me that anymore."

"You go by several names; isn't that right?"

"Well, yes. I was called Clay when I was young to distinguish me from my father and grandfather."

"But you are not one of them. I already knew that. You came here for a reason, Clay. You have to return this to her." And she took off the bracelet and handed it to him.

"Return it to whom? Who do I need to give it to, and why?"

"Too many questions, Clay. You will know when the time is right." Then she leaned even closer and whispered in a raspy voice, "*She belongs to me, and therefore I belong to you.*"

Michael was completely puzzled and didn't understand a thing she had said. "How will I know her? What if I give it to the wrong person?"

"You will know. She will call you by your childhood name."

Michael began having doubts, now. This must be a con. It had to be. "How much?"

"What do you mean?" she asked softly.

"How much are you soaking me for this bracelet that, most likely, is a fake?"

"Oh, Clay, you insult me so. There is no price on true and everlasting love. Take it. It is yours. It is the reason you are here. And there's no reason to return to London again. The one whom you are seeking will not change her mind."

It was too much. She knew everything. Michael was in shock. "Oh, I see. Well – um – well, I'd better go. I'm late. What do I owe you for the – uh – reading?"

"Your presence is all that I required. Take the crystal ball to Ivy and give her my best regards." Michael gasped. She winked and handed him her card. 'Seer of all Things. Fortune Teller – Gina.'

Chapter Five

On the ride back to the hotel, Michael kept his hand in his pocket running his fingers over the blue stones of the bracelet. She had not wrapped it or given him a receipt. For all he knew, it could be stolen, and she was pawning it off on him before she got caught. He wondered all the way back if he should go to the police and report it. But report what? That he had stumbled into a fortune telling shop and a mysterious woman simply gave him what looked to be a very expensive bracelet? Who would believe that? He would probably be suspected as the thief himself. No, it was better to keep quiet. He decided to take it to a pawn shop or jewelry store and see if they could evaluate it for him. But then he thought if it was stolen, he would end up in jail, rotting away in jolly old England. Should he throw it away and never look back at his crazy experience? 'Think,' he told himself, 'think.'

The cabbie arrived at his hotel, parking in front in a space reserved for guests. The doorman quickly opened the car door for him, while holding an umbrella over his head. Michael threw some money at the driver, not even bothering to figure out if the tip was correct, then he practically ran all the way to his room where he locked the door behind him. Once he was alone, he breathed a sigh of relief. He had made it. No one was chasing him. After taking a few deep breaths to calm himself, he took out the bracelet to give it a good look in bright light. It was truly an amazing piece of jewelry, and if it was fake, it was a darn good one. It was approximately one inch wide and held four rows of diamonds running around the entire bracelet. The outside rows were the anchors and were straight, but the two inside rows moved like a river, bending with the current. In between the rows was a blend of small, medium, and large sapphires, evenly spaced, but in a random pattern. The bracelet was so well made it felt like a flexible mesh. It was meant to conform to a woman's wrist, move easily with her gestures, and not get caught on her sleeve. This was not a cheap piece of jewelry. Real stones or not, it was well-made and looked as if it had been around for a very long time. It could use a gentle cleaning, but that was it.

Michael played with the bracelet a few moments, feeling the weight of it, wondering how in the world he would be able to get it through customs if he took it back. He did not have a single piece of paper or document for it. He thought of mailing it to himself, but then there was always a risk of it being stolen. He laughed out loud. He was probably holding stolen jewelry right now, and he was worried about someone stealing it from him! Michael was just about to get rid of the thing, toss it in the waste basket, when he remembered all the things this Gina knew about him. She knew he was adopted, she knew he went by Clay when he was young, and she knew he was looking for his mother, she even called Ivy by name. Maybe he should pay attention to the rest of what she had to say. It sounded like he was to save this bauble and give it to the woman he fell in love with, and not just any woman, but a particular woman he didn't even know yet. He had to admit that it was intriguing. If she was half as beautiful as the gypsy he had just met, he could easily spend the rest of his life with her. In fact a girl of that very description had been dancing in his dreams for as long as he could remember. A gypsy but not a gypsy. A nymph on a lake with long hair and a luxurious body. A temptress.

In the end, Michael decided to keep the bracelet. He decided to hire a private jet and perhaps that way, he would have less trouble with Customs. And that's exactly what he did the following morning. He left the bracelet in his pocket and decided if it was discovered, he would pretend he had forgotten it was there. Didn't they say, it was better to beg for forgiveness than ask for permission? With his heart pounding, he went through x-ray and oddly enough, nothing was detected. He almost passed out, but continued on. Once he got on his jet, he collapsed in a ball of sweat. Obviously, he was not meant to be an undercover agent or an international spy. He couldn't handle the pressure. He relaxed a little as soon as the jet was in the air. The flight was uneventful, but when he arrived in the U.S., he knew he would have to go through the same thing again. Strangely enough, for the second time, nothing unusual was detected. Perhaps the thing was plastic.

He had left his car at the airport long-term lot, so he strolled across the expanse of parked cars, quickly got into his waiting silver BMW, and locked the doors. He couldn't get home soon enough.

∞

It had been over a week since Michael's trip to London. The bracelet was locked away in the wall safe. He had hoped 'out of sight, out of mind' would help, but that had not worked. He still thought of it constantly.

He wanted so badly to take it to a jewelers for appraisal, but then at least one person, other than himself, would know he had it. It was best if it was kept locked away. Nothing could go wrong if he never held it in his hands.

There were two things Michael wanted to accomplish next, and it had nothing to do with London, his biological mother, or gypsies. His small mansion on the lake was in great condition, and thanks to the renovations that had been done, it had all of the modern amenities, but it was lacking in furniture and decorative style. It needed some personality. He had been referred to an interior designer by the real estate agent who had sold him the house, so after finding her card in a folder with the deed and insurance papers, he had placed a call. They agreed to meet before he went abroad, and he had placed an order with her for window treatments and furniture, giving her free reign once he was sure she knew his taste. She was also shopping for color coordinated towels for the bathrooms, sheets for the beds, and artwork for the walls. Today, he needed to place a call to see how things were coming; he was anxious to be done with the decorating and just live, because once it was all done, he was planning on throwing a party for his friends.

After making contact with Sheryl, the designer, he was assured that everything would be delivered over the course of this week. Then she would need a day or two to make adjustments and place everything in its proper position. There were always some items, when doing a job of this size, that seemed right on paper, but did not hold up to her standards when they were in the house, she told him. She said it was best to wait until they were completely finished before planning his open house. Time delays were inevitable.

Michael walked out to his patio which was sparsely furnished with a few woven webbed, lawn chairs. He sat for a while and looked at the lake. It was actually quite still today. On days like this, when there was a light wind and clear sky, the white sails of the boats were a sight to behold. There was a time when Muskegon Lake was a hub of activity. Large freighters came through the channel from Lake Michigan on a daily basis, delivering iron ore for the many foundries that had been built along the shoreline. After Muskegon's lumber business faded out, due to over-harvesting the trees, the city almost collapsed. But at the same time, the use of the horse and buggy for transportation was slowly being replaced as people turned to cars, and cars were built in Michigan. Automobiles and trucks were highly desired, and it was impossible to keep up with the demand. Building vehicles required steel and iron, and many other automotive parts. Factories began to pop up all over, and Muskegon became a major supplier for Detroit's car factories. Besides iron and steel, it built everything from piston rings to gas pumps to engine blocks. The entire automotive industry kept everyone in jobs. But this era took a toll on the city as the smoke stacks rose to spew out their filth in the sky.

Eventually, in 1970, when the Clean Air Act was passed, the beauty of Muskegon slowly began to come back. But the other side of the coin was that the new act was hard on the workers and their jobs. Cars were being built by machines and robots, people lost jobs, and no one had any money to buy cars of their own. It was a vicious cycle that seemed to have no end. The city lost its spark altogether. Over time, and a lot of forward-thinking council members, people looked to the lakes and rivers as a tourist industry for fishing, swimming, and pleasure boating. The beaches were the attraction. A renaissance was born. Today, Michael watched as the beautiful white car ferry left the dock and crossed the 118 mile expanse of Lake Michigan to Wisconsin, heavily loaded with cars and people, but still moving gracefully across the long stretch of dangerous waves. It blasted its departure call which echoed over the water. Later this evening the dinner cruise boat would tour the lake, travel through the channel to the mouth of Lake Michigan, and reverse its route to return to the dock after an evening of dinner and dance.

Always inquisitive, Michael wondered what it must have been like here before all of the people came – when the flora and fauna were wild and abundant, when the geese flew in such thick flocks you could barely see the sky, when deer nibbled on the grasses with no fear except for an occasional Indian's arrow, when fishing was so easy from the rivers and streams a fisherman simply had to drop in a line and pull something up or take his pick from the huge schools of Northern pike with a spear. It would have been like that when Father Jacques Marquette, the French priest, who had converted many tribes to Christianity, passed through along with his friend, the explorer Louis Joliet. Michael had been researching them both as they would be the subject of his upcoming book about the history of Michigan. He was just in the beginning stages, but he could envision them paddling along this lake in their canoes, stopping to spend the night on the bank, cooking fresh fish over a campfire, and sharing a meal with the natives. It must have been an incredible time to live, he thought. He stretched his long legs and breathed deeply of the fresh night air, knowing that he could not begin to understand what it must have smelled like before human beings had put their industrial mark on the area. There was both good and bad, now, but nothing could be done to reverse things at this stage. Progress had come too far, and once it had taken hold, it would not be stopped.

Chapter Six

They were finally gone, so she had the house all to herself. It was the first time she had been left alone here. She had been living with her sister and her brother-in-law for over six months now, but she usually just came and went on her own accord. This time she would be trusted with the responsibilities of running a house. Marge and Ken had left her with a long list of instructions. She needed to make sure the underground sprinkling came on at proper intervals; it had been acting up lately. The repairman's number was on the kitchen counter along with all other necessary contact information. She needed to make sure she locked the French doors to the patio when she left the house. They were the easy ones to forget when you were late and running out the door, they said. "And please, just toss the mail in the basket I left out. I'll take care of it all when I get back," said Marge. "It's most likely junk, anyway, but you never know. So keep it all." Her sister could be so anal.

"Yes, I will be sure to do that," she responded.

"And take Tessie out for a long walk at least twice a day. She'll need quick trips more often. I know her droppings are small, but they need to be picked up from the lawn promptly. The lawn care service comes on Thursdays, and I would prefer that they don't run over any of it."

"Yes, I understand." She was writing everything down on a tablet. She had a perfectly good memory, but she wanted Marge to know she was serious and taking it all in, which she was, of course. But even though Marge always thought of her as the irresponsible younger sister, she was anything but. They just had different ways of doing things; they always had. Where Marge was more of a social butterfly, much like their mother, Emmy was serious and quiet. She followed her grandmother's traits; they were both deep thinkers and seemed to have a knowledge of the world that others did not comprehend.

"And under no circumstances is Tessie allowed to go out without a leash. There's too much chance for her to get lost in those bushes along the side yard. There are thistles under there that need to be cleaned out."

"Of course. Got it." She quickly jotted more notes on her tablet.

Emmaline said she would care for the small Shih Tzu like it was her own. It would be easy, because she loved Tessie Cheng. She was sweet and lovable, and she never got into any trouble. In fact, she rarely barked; sometimes it was difficult to tell what she wanted, because she would sit and stare at her owners instead of begging for food or asking to go out. She was an odd dog, but extremely sweet. She would make a great companion in this very, large, stately home.

And finally, after more last minute instructions, and lots of kisses on Tessie's small head, and hugs between the three of them, she stood on the doorstep and waved goodbye as Marge and Ken left for their four-month cruise around the world. Emmy closed the door behind them and sighed. She leaned against the door frame and looked at her surroundings. The tall ceilings of the foyer went all the way up to the second floor. The staircase came straight down in the middle, growing wider as it approached the floor and then curving back on each side as it wrapped around the newel posts. Her sister had married well, especially since she had never held a good paying job in her life. 'Someday,' she thought, 'I will own something like this. I just know it. But I'll get it on my own.' The big question was how. She was a school teacher, and was recently hired into the local school system, but only as a substitute. That was all they had to offer at the moment. She was scheduled to start in the fall.

Emmy hugged herself and spun around in circles as she danced on the parquet floor to music that she heard in her head. As she started to hum, Tessie joined in the fun and began spinning in circles at her feet. Emmy laughed at the little fluff ball, picked her up, and carried her to the patio, but first she stopped at the door to hook up the leash. It would not do to get off to a bad start on her first day.

∞

It was Saturday, so Michael decided to take a trip into town, as he usually did on the last day of the week. He wanted to stop at the library to get a few more books, and then he thought he might stroll through the farmer's market. For some reason, being around fresh vegetables and fruits always made him feel mellow, and he needed that right now. Normally, that's exactly who he was, mellow, but since the sapphire bracelet had come into his possession, he was uneasy – always wondering what to expect next. Gina had done that to him. He figured if he was not holding the jewels, there was probably no chance of meeting this person he was supposed to meet, but he could hardly walk around with a bracelet full of gemstones in his pocket. On the other hand, hadn't the gypsy, Gina, said he needed to give it to the one he loved? She never said it was meant to find her. He supposed the meeting part was up to him. But where? At the library? The farmer's market? Those were the only places he normally went, unless he was with the guys watching a game on TV. Michael sighed. Maybe he should forget about this whole thing. No one would know if he gave up on the idea. He hadn't breathed a word of it to anyone; it was too bizarre.

After running his errands, Michael came home with a stack of books under his arm, and a bagful of vegetables. He dropped the food items on his new kitchen counter, then rinsed off a McIntosh apple; he enjoyed the sound of the popping peel as he took his first bite. The apple was a slight bit tart and very juicy, just the way he liked it. He dabbed at a bit of juice that had escaped his lips and was trickling down his chin, then he placed his books on the table next to the computer. As soon as he changed his clothes, he planned on digging into them while he sat on the patio.

The new Adirondack furniture had finally arrived. It was time he took it for a test run. He had specifically requested thick cushions to cover the white wooden slats. The decorator had done well. None of those bright beachy colors for him, he had said. He loved the way the brown was swirled with rust and forest green on the tufted seat pads. The deep gold umbrella for the glass-top table coordinated perfectly with the chairs; the colors were echoed in the outdoor plates and napkins stashed away in the kitchen. It was manly and suited his taste.

He climbed the stairs slowly, admiring his house once again. The view from the second floor bedroom was his favorite place. It looked directly south onto the water, which was sparkling and clear today, so blue it reminded him of the bracelet hidden away in the wall of this very room. Michael opened a French door and stepped out onto the balcony. He leaned on the railing and watched the boats for a few minutes, totally lost in what must be happening out there. He imagined families taking a leisurely cruise and then docking on a sandy beach for a picnic. He imagined men heading out to fish in the big lake, outfitted with outriggers, downriggers, radar, GPS, chart plotters, and fish finders; all so they could bring home a few fish for dinner. Of course, he knew that often big deals were made on these boats, as friendships were forged over their bonding experience. He had done it himself. And maybe, he thought, one of the boats which had cabins with a galley and bedrooms below deck, was being used at this very moment – two people entwined in their own rocking motion matching the roll of the waves, their oil-slicked bodies hot from the sun. Michael chuckled to himself. He must be getting lonely, if his mind was going in that direction.

Just then his eye caught a movement. He had not noticed before that he could see right into the backyard of his neighbor's house. A woman was bent over as she worked at hooking up a small dog to a leash attached to a screw-in anchor in the grass. She had her back to him, but she seemed to be fairly young -- maybe in her twenties or thirties. She had dark hair twisted up in a clip, and a long flowing sundress with thin straps. It moved around her body conforming to her figure as she bent to talk to the dog. He couldn't hear anything she said, but it was obvious she was fond of her pet. She sat in her lounge chair, facing away from him, and then she gracefully crossed her legs at the ankle, pulling her dress up above her knees to expose them to the sun. He caught a flash of gold – she must be wearing an ankle bracelet. His eyes followed the leather thongs of the sandals as they traveled upwards, wrapping around her calves. From this distance her legs looked quite shapely. Michael was intrigued, more than intrigued. He was already in a daydream about who she was, and who she belonged to, if anyone. He wondered what it would be like to be close to her; what color were her eyes? Did she smell like warm suntan lotion or cool, fresh, summer rain? When she shifted in her chair, he suddenly realized he was being a voyeur. It would not be a good start if he was caught. He turned his head and pulled his eyes away, then slowly stepped back into the house. Maybe if he got downstairs quickly enough, he could say hello. It was always a good thing to be friendly with your neighbors, wasn't it? Yes, that's what he would do.

Forgetting to change his clothes, he hurried downstairs, grabbed a book, so he would look casual, and slowed his steps as he wandered out into the yard. Unfortunately, he had not realized until this very moment that the privet hedge was too tall and thick for him to see next door, which was no doubt the reason for it in the first place. It was a privacy wall. Feeling a little let down, he consoled himself with the fact that she lived right on the other side of the blasted, tall, green thing. He would meet her eventually, he supposed, so he carried his book back inside to his computer and began his research on Father Marquette.

∞

Emmy couldn't get enough of the outdoors and this luxurious setting. She was out here almost every day that the sun was shining. She stretched her body out in its warm rays. Glad for the tall hedge, she hiked her dress up a little higher, exposing her perfectly shaped thighs. No one could see her, so she had no worries about her lack of coverage. She had complete privacy, unless someone was down by the dock. Then they could easily see up the lawn, straight to the patio.

After living in a small apartment for a while, she had finally run out of money. Her sister had begged her to come and live with them on the lake. She said they had more than enough room, and she would love the company when Ken was out of town. Marge pleaded that Emmy could help out with Tessie when they were on vacation. The Thompsons loved the little Shih Tzu so much that Marge almost didn't want to go on her anniversary cruise, because she would have to leave her dog behind. She only agreed to the trip after Emmy had moved in.

Emmy's thoughts were interrupted by a cardinal's shrill call, which was followed by a chickadee's tweet. Enjoying the birdcalls, Emmy settled back into her chair.

The breeze off the lake caressed her body and lulled her into a gentle doze. The book she held on her lap slipped precariously to the side, almost dropping to the patio floor. She could hear the gulls heralding their friends over the lake, and the katydids humming their electric-sounding drone. Tessie gave a short little bark, probably at a grasshopper, or a leaf moving out of her reach. A fly landed on Emmy's leg, so she moved her ankle to brush it off without opening her eyes; it was followed by an irritating tickle which was persistent on her cheek. She jumped, thinking it could be a bee, but when she peeked out, she saw a handsome blonde man standing over her. A slow grin spread over her face.

"Hey, beautiful," he said, then he bent over her and kissed her as he pulled her up to a standing position. She wrapped her arms around his neck, and returned the kiss with longing. A slow, sensuous smile played on her lips, but then she pulled back with a gasp.

"How did you get in?"

"I rang the bell, but when you didn't answer, I walked around to the back. The gate wasn't locked. Shame on you."

"Oh, boy. I forgot to check that one. There are so many locks on this place, that I can't remember them all."

"Well, you'd better start, or I might have to move in, in order to protect you." He slapped her playfully on the butt.

"Daniel, cut that out. You know I don't like that."

"Well, you deserved it. You're not safe here alone. If you would let me move in, I could be here daily to protect you. You know I'm crazy about you. I just don't want anything to happen to my girl."

"But *you* know that I promised not to have any live-in boyfriends, or any live-in friends at all. Marge trusted me to take care of the house, Danny. You know I can't risk getting kicked out. I don't have a regular paycheck, yet."

"Sure, I get it. But it's hard, you know. I want to see you all the time. I want to be with you all the time."

He pulled her in again, tight to his body, and as his hands began to roam, he rocked her to an unsung melody. She smiled and then untangled herself from his hands, bent down to unhook Tessie, then took his hand and walked them both inside.

∞

A frown creased Michael's brow; he was ashamed of himself. He had not meant to watch again the next day, but it was almost impossible not to. She was out there all the time, and his curiosity was out of control. He had begun to have dreams about the woman next door; she had merged into the vision that had haunted him for years. But now it was obvious that she was taken, and more than that, probably married. She was very familiar with the man that was there on the patio with her. He had been there several times now. Michael longed to be in his place, but now he would have to give up that dream. It would be difficult, because he felt such a strong connection to her, even though he had not even seen her face. It was time to get out and meet more people. This infatuation had to stop.

His house warming party was this weekend. Maybe someone would bring a guest that he could get to know, or maybe they would suggest introducing him to someone new. If not, he would just come out with it and ask one of the guys if they knew someone they could hook him up with. Until then, it was back to his research. He would have to be content with the history and explorers of Michigan. Maybe one of them had a love life he would enjoy reading about.

Chapter Seven

The house party was finally happening. With the help of a caterer, all the food had been prepared in advance. Drinks were mixed under a small canopy in a grassy area. It looked like the bartender really knew his stuff. He spun bottles like they were six-shooters from the Old West. He poured from up high and behind his back to complete the show. Finger foods of many kinds were on the tables to stave off hunger, while the grill was being manned by a professional chef. He was cooking up enough steaks and burgers for an army. Michael had held nothing back. Edison lights, Chinese lanterns, and

Tiki torches were placed around the yard for later in the evening when it began to get dark. It was to be an all-day affair, with swimming and boating for everyone. Michael had rented some paddle boats, a few jet skis, and kayaks for his guests' pleasure. Money was no object.

He was more than pleased to see that everyone he had invited had arrived on time and was eager to start the fun. Ivy and Fox came with their kids, Ruby and Sal. Ivy was not showing her pregnancy yet, but from what he had heard, she was carrying a little Maisy who would arrive sometime in the early spring. Paul and Connie brought little Jackie, who was just as cute as a button, his round plump face always smiling. Georgy and Jack arrived next, holding hands and just as much in love as ever. The wedding was planned for next summer, and it couldn't come soon enough for them, they said. Sue and Duane were next to ring the doorbell, followed by Rob and Rosie. That relationship looked like it was going well, too. It was good to see Rob so healthy after the kidney transplant. Michael looked at his group of friends and couldn't feel more blessed. He had truly stumbled into something wonderful the day he went to the family research class.

There wasn't much time for a meaningful conversation throughout most of the day, just a lot of teasing and camaraderie. The horseshoe pit was in use all afternoon, the pleasant clink of the shoes echoing over the lake. Corn Hole, the popular summer lawn game, was also available for those who preferred a gentler toss game. But most of all there was laughter and lots of splashing in the water.

Towards the end of the day Michael finally had a chance to sit down and rest. He had not realized just how difficult being a host was. It had seemed he was always getting somebody something or showing someone around his house, so when he finally found himself seated across from Ivy and Fox, he grabbed the gift he had brought Ivy from London.

"I wanted to thank you for bringing us all together, Ivy, so I brought you something from England."

"What? Oh no, it was Georgy's class that brought us together. I had nothing to do with that."

"But you had us out to your house for a picnic, and that forged our bonds beyond what we had in common in the class. It was kind of you both, and meant a lot to me, since I was new here."

"Well, thank you, Michael. Let me see what you brought me, though it really wasn't necessary." She giggled like a child on her birthday. "I have to admit, I do love getting a gift." Pulling the wrapping off carefully, she peeked inside, but found only a non-descript box. When she pulled out the crystal ball, she smiled broadly, immediately recognizing the significance. "Oh, Michael, it's beautiful. And that was so kind of you."

"As soon as I saw it, I immediately thought of you."

"Where did you find such a thing?" she asked, simply out of curiosity.

"That is a tale for another day, I'm afraid. Maybe we'll have a chat when there aren't so many people around."

Fox raised an eyebrow, and Ivy said slowly, "Okay. Whenever you want to talk, I'm available. Will this make a good story for me?"

"It just might," replied Michael. "We'll have to wait and see."

"Hmm," added Fox, "intriguing. Not to change the subject, but I must add that you have done a marvelous job on the house. You know I was the inspector for the original sale."

"Yes, you worked for Piper Evans, right?"

"Yes, I did. There was a lot that had to be done at that time to get it up to code."

"She took care of most of it, as a condition of the sale, and then I had the rest taken care of after I purchased it. We went right off your list."

"How do you like it here?" asked Ivy.

"I love it. I feel right at home."

"Have you had a chance to meet your neighbors?" asked Fox, carefully.

"Not yet. The driveways are long, and as you can see, the hedge prevents me from seeing over. So I never see anyone out here," lied Michael. He wondered why he had said that. Maybe it was because he was ashamed of the way he had been watching the neighbors.

"Well, good luck."

"What do you mean by that?"

"I should not be telling tales, I know it's not professional, but the Thompsons can be a bit trying. They gave us some problems with our work trucks, etc."

"The Thompsons? They're married, then?"

"Yes, they are and have been for several years, but I'm sure you'll get to know each other in due time. I'm sure you'll get along just fine. There's always an adjustment when someone new comes into the neighborhood."

Fox saw the look that crossed over Michael's face. Was it disappointment or surprise? He wasn't sure, because Michael's expression was fleeting, and then the conversation moved to the children who were in a small spat; one of them had begun to wail.

'She's married,' he thought. 'That's that, then.' Michael would never think about crossing that line.

'And what's wrong with me, anyway,' he wondered. 'I've yet to see her face.'

∞

There was a party going on next door to the Thompsons' house. Emmy was a little irritated, but she supposed that was life on a lake. She took Tessie for her walks out the front door and down the block so she could do her 'duty'; otherwise, the little social butterfly would only people-watch, staring at what was going on down by the docks. Boats were coming and going, people were laughing and shrieking at times, and the smell of the grilled food was making Emmy salivate. She wished her sister had allowed her to have a small party of her own. They were far, far away, and would never know if she had one anyway, but she didn't want to risk her free living arrangement. For all she knew, they probably had neighborhood spies planted everywhere.

Emmy went inside, closed the doors and windows, and turned on the air conditioner. She decided to take this time to get some reading done. She had a pile the size of a mountain next to her bed. Last night in the wee hours, she had finished the novel she was reading. It wasn't too interesting, but she never quit a book. Her theory was that you never knew when it would turn around and become your favorite of all time, but that had not happened in this case. The story was slow moving and boring. 'Such a waste of time', she thought.

Emmy grabbed the top book on her pile, picked up Tessie, and put her on the bed, which was fine with the small dog. Tessie wanted nothing more than to be near her at all times; she was feeling a little lost without her mistress. She curled up close to Emmy's leg and settled into the soft covers. The night was young, so Emmy had plenty of time to see if this book was any better than the last. She had purchased it at the suggestion of a school teacher friend. It was written by a local author and had been getting good reviews, and best of all, it was a series. Emmy loved digging into long family sagas.

"Okay," the young woman said aloud, "Let's see what this is about. Hmm? Ruby and Sal. Good title, huh, Tessie? What do you think? No comment? Okay, we'll talk later."

It turned out that Ruby and Sal was so good she could not put it down. Reading well into the night, Emmy finally had to get up to put on her night clothes, and wash her face. The nightly ritual was the worst, but because she had always taken care with her creams and lotions, her skin glowed. She was proud of her complexion, but she had to admit that it probably came from her heritage, and had nothing to do with all of her effort. It was all in her genes – DNA. She came from good peasant stock, Grandma Kezzie used to say. One side of her family went back for generations to the Ukraine. Her grandmother loved to talk about her mother, a Ukrainian gypsy. Whenever her grandmother told those stories, she watched Emmy's face closely, and she always saw awe and wonderment in the young girl.

Strangely enough, Grandma had no interest in Marge. When Emmy was young she wondered why Grandma didn't care for Marge, but as Emmy grew older, it only took a look in the mirror to see how she resembled her grandmother's side of the family, which explained it all. Marge looked more like their father, and she had his temperament, too – uptight and demanding. Emmy usually let things roll off her back, always sure that tomorrow would be a better day. Where Marge was fair, Emmy was dark. Marge freckled in the sun and burned easily, but Emmy tanned a golden brown. Marge had an athletic build, but Emmy was slender and willowy. Marge was pretty in a cute sort of way, but Emmy was drop dead gorgeous.

Marge was a few years older than Emmy, so she started dating first, but once the boys came to the house and spotted her younger sister, it was all over. They lost their interest in Marge, because even though Emmy was only twelve, the sixteen-year-old boys couldn't keep their eyes off of her. She had already developed a graceful walk and self-confidence that was appealing to the opposite sex. Her long dark hair would swing as she moved through the house; she had a natural magnetic charm, and because she ignored them, it made her all the more alluring.

Once Marge figured out what was happening, she made sure that Emmy was not around when she brought a new boy home, and she began to spend more time at her friends' homes. As Emmy grew up to be a gorgeous young woman with a sex appeal that was undeniable to men, Marge became more and more jealous. Then one day she 'snagged', as she called it, a handsome, rich man, and she felt she finally had the upper hand. Ken, many years older than Marge, was thrilled with his match. He loved Marge and promised he would give her anything she wanted, and she eagerly took him up on that. It wasn't until she was totally sure of him, and did not see any sign of interest in Emmy, that she let her sister move in with them. Ken confessed that he had always been attracted to light-haired women, and Emmy's dark exotic looks were of no interest to him whatsoever. 'In fact,' he told Marge in private, 'your sister puts me off a bit. It seems as though she can look right through me, and it makes me very uncomfortable.'

Marge knew exactly what he was talking about. She had seen it first-hand. Her sister had the same ability as their grandmother – she could read things about people, see things that even they weren't aware of. Maybe it was an instinct on watching body language, or maybe she could read people's minds, but it could be frightening at times, especially for a teenage girl who was sneaking out of her bedroom to meet a boy in the middle of the night. Emmy always knew when she was lying to their parents, and often threatened to tell. It unnerved her. But now Marge felt secure in her role as wife to a prominent man, and she no longer worried about Emmy taking him away; besides, this long trip would keep them all apart for a good long time. When they got back, Emmy could go her own way, and find another place to live, and Marge would once again be the lady of the house and the ruler of her domain.

Chapter Eight

The yard was cleaned up, to a point. Nothing was left out that could blow away in the wind. The kitchen was fairly decent. Sleeping children had been carried out to the cars, and goodbyes were said. The sound of the last car leaving the driveway left him feeling hollow. Michael was alone in his house, and after the events of the day, it seemed far too empty.

As always happened to him after an active day, he could not sleep. He turned over and over remembering bits of conversation. He had so wanted to get Ivy off in a corner somewhere and grill her on that necklace she had written about. It just had too many similarities to his bracelet to be fiction, but the time was never right. Every time he saw an opening, or had some time from the lively chaos, they were interrupted. He decided he would set up a meeting with her where they could talk in private. Michael rolled the words around in his head as to what he would say to her without sounding like an idiot. He knew she wrote fiction, but sometimes fiction reflected real life. He needed to find out if it did in her case.

Michael sat up from his bed and placed his feet on the cool tile floor, then he walked to the safe and turned the dial, listening to the clicks until the door popped open. He stared inside a moment, wondering if he was a fool to believe in anything he had been told by the gypsy in London; besides, it didn't really make sense. He gingerly pulled out the small velvet bag and dumped the bracelet into his hand. It was cold to the touch, but other than that there was nothing out of the ordinary, other than the beauty of the gems. Rolling his fingers over the stones, he walked toward the French doors to the balcony and stepped out into the damp night air. There was a fog rolling in; the moon was covered with a soft wisp as if someone had been smoking and had blown a trail of smoke up to the sky, but even in the low light, the sapphires and diamonds sparkled beyond belief. They were truly incredible. Michael had read somewhere that if in doubt whether jewels were real or not, to clink them on your teeth. A soft thud detected plastic or man-made material; a gentle clink was stone or some type of natural substance. Also, anything cold was of the earth, because it was not able to hold heat. Man-made substances picked up the temperature of their surroundings. His bracelet was not only cold, but there was a nice clinking sound when he tapped it on his lower teeth. Standing here in the soft moonlight, he was sure these stones were one hundred percent authentic.

Suddenly, a single spark emanated from the bracelet, shooting over the railing; the surprise of it almost caused Michael to drop the gems. That was the first time anything had happened since he was in the shop in London. Michael turned it over and over to see if there was some sort of battery in the thing, but he knew better. He had already gone through this detailed search in the house and in better light. It was just a bracelet. Nothing more. But then another spark and another shot out into the darkness. It seemed to be sputtering to life. Afraid he would drop it over the edge, he stepped back in and with shaking hands placed the sapphires back in the safe. He almost felt like he was putting away a friend, but he had no other choice but to secure it in this way. Walking back to the open French door, he began to lock it, and as he did so, he thought he caught a movement down below. He quietly stepped back out on the balcony. It was now quite dark, a foggy haze was covering the yard, but as he studied the lot for a while, he could see nothing out of the ordinary, until he caught a glimpse of a naked woman twirling in the moonlight. The haze covered her body for the most part, but there was no doubt she was dancing totally naked. Her face was illusive, and her long hair covered most of her private parts, but on one of her twirls, he was able to catch a quick view of firm breasts and a well-rounded derriere. No, it was wrong, he thought. It was a complete violation of privacy. He shook his head, coughed lightly, and went to bed. This time he quickly fell asleep, where he dreamed of an elusive dark-haired nymph who emerged from the lake, tempting him to follow, and before he had a chance to do so, she disappeared in the fog.

∞

Emmy couldn't sleep. She had tried, but only tossed and turned. She removed her pajamas, because she much preferred sleeping naked anyway, and just lying there waiting for the elusive trip to dreamland wasn't helping anything. She simply wasn't ready to close her eyes for the night. She decided maybe she needed a little fresh air; she never had been one for air conditioning, but the humidity had been oppressive lately, and it was the only escape. She put on her fluffy slippers, wrapped her naked body in a filmy robe, and went outside. Tessie wasn't happy; she had wanted to follow, but Emmy thought it was too dangerous to take her out in the fog. If she lost that dog, her sister would never forgive her. The fog had been hovering over the lake, but now it was moving inland quickly. A single wisp floated over the moon. Emmy watched as the houses around the lake disappeared from view, one after another, as they were covered with a cloak of gray. It was magical and mystical, and it tugged at something deep in her core. It took her back to when she was a child. She had always loved playing in fog, spinning and twirling until she could no longer stand. Suddenly, she had the urge to spin once again in that same childlike way, but this time a little slower, and so she began to dance. She wanted to connect with the earth and sky. She wanted to be transported out of her body. Daniel wasn't much for dancing; he only did it when she asked. But here, alone, when no one was watching, she felt free again. She threw back her head, her hair hanging down her back, and slowly twirled with her arms out. The tie of her robe came undone with her movements and her robe opened, but she didn't care. With a smile on her face, she danced with seductive movements for the Man in the Moon. Was that shock that she saw on his face? It looked like he was saying "Oh!" A small laugh escaped. It was so good to be unencumbered of her worries, that she dropped the robe altogether. Oh, how Marge would be scandalized to know her sister was dancing all alone in her backyard under the moon's powdery glow, with nothing on but what the Good Lord had given her. As the dampness touched her skin, she was washed in nature's finest moisturizer, adding a dewy softness to her already velvety skin.

Emmy was startled by a soft sound; she thought she detected a movement from above. Yes, it sounded like a click of a door and a scrape of a shoe. She glanced over her shoulder, but she could see nothing through the fog; then she heard a light cough or clearing of the throat. Someone was up there next door, on the balcony. Had he or she been watching her? She grabbed her robe and quickly retreated inside. As she ran toward the house, she looked up. She could not even see the railing up above, so she reasoned if she couldn't see them, then they couldn't see her. Relief spread over her. It would not do to upset Marge just because she had felt the need to purify herself in the mist. Marge already thought she was strange enough. There was no reason to give her any more ammunition, so she could find a reason to expel her from this house. Emmy had really settled in and for some reason felt a strong connection to her new home. She sighed and crawled back into bed, with Tessie nuzzled in at her side. She was ready for sleep now. With one slow deep breath, she quickly drifted off to a dream of moving water. A handsome man was calling her. What was he saying? What was that? And then she went under the waves and left him behind.

Chapter Nine

The morning hours brought a cool, refreshing, new world. The sun was shining through a crystal clear sky, and it looked to be an idyllic day. Michael felt renewed after his sleep filled with dreams of the unknown woman. He was always happiest when she visited him in his fantasy world. She must be the one chosen for him, the one his bracelet would lead him to, but how and when? He needed to get out of the house and move among people; it was the only way. He would never find her here.

After a quick shower and an even quicker breakfast, he left to take a walk along the channel. There were a few early souls walking with their spouses and partners. He seemed to be the only lone duck taking a stroll. He wouldn't find her here today. It was one more jab in his heart. From this side of the channel, he could look at the coast guard station and the lighthouse on the Muskegon side. It never ceased to impress him. A few fishing boats putting slowly in the no-wake zone, along with two sailboats which were quietly gliding to the bigger lake, caused a small ripple of water, but for the most part, the channel was quite still.

Michael picked up his pace, and after a brisk walk along the boardwalk, he found an unoccupied bench that seemed to be calling his name. He sat down, and breathed in the fresh air, slightly pungent with fish, and imagined how it must have been when Father Jacques Marquette and Louis Joliet first explored this region. This is the area of study Michael had been working on for his book. How brave these men must have been to venture into unknown territory in 1672.

Father Marquette was a French missionary in Sault Ste. Marie in 1669, but in 1671 he started a missionary in St. Ignace. The entire area, called New France was controlled by the French government. It stretched all the way from Newfoundland to the Great Lakes and down toward the Gulf of Mexico. Establishing their Catholic church in the new territory was of utmost importance to the French government. Father Marquette already had a great rapport with, and respect for, the different Indian tribes in the area, so he slowly began to convert the natives to his faith.

In 1672 Father Jacques Marquette set out with Louis Joliet to explore for their country. Joliet's mission was to create a new-world map and the priest's mission was to bring as many heathens as possible to Christianity. With only five canoes and a handful of men, they traveled south on Lake Michigan's east coast, across to Wisconsin, and then down the Mississippi River toward Louisiana. They only turned back when they were told that the Spanish were coming north on the same river. Not wanting a confrontation they headed back the way they had come. Each man carefully documented their journey, but Joliet's diary was lost when it fell overboard in rough water. Father Marquette's journal was all that was left to tell the stories of their trip.

Along the return journey Father Marquette became very ill with dysentery. It was his wish to get back to St. Ignace to his mission, but the small group had to halt their progress in what is modern day Ludington, for he was too sick to go on, and that is where the priest took his last breath in 1675. He was buried there with a small marker, but a few years later his loyal followers moved his body to the chapel at his mission in St. Ignace. His journal describing this previously unknown territory was instrumental in aiding many other explorers. The knowledge he gained as an explorer was important, but even more so were the contacts and friends he made with the native people. He converted many souls, and was loved by all. By the end of his life he had learned six of their languages.

"Excuse me, may I sit here? It seems to be the only bench with any seating available."

Michael was shocked out of his reverie. He jumped at the sound of a female voice. "Sure, no problem." He scooted over to give her room, and then looked up to see who he was talking to. It was impossible to see her face. She wore a wide-brimmed hat; her hair which was tucked up underneath it, looked dark at the nape of her neck. Huge sunglasses covered her eyes, but her voice was like music to his ears. She wore long dangling earrings with delicate chains that had some silver stars at the end of them. Each star had a sparkling sapphire in the center of it.

She laughed, and it was then he noticed that she had a small dog on a leash. It was a fluffy little thing, all white with dark ears and a few darker patches on her body.

"And who is this?" he asked, as he reached out to pet the friendly puppy.

"This is Tessie."

"She's very cute."

"And she knows it, believe me. Is that an English accent I detect?"

"Yes, but it's a long story. I was raised in England until I was 13, and then we came to America. I've been a resident here for almost 15 years, but I've never been able to drop the accent."

She leaned closer and actually bumped into his shoulder. The contact was shocking. "Don't ever lose it. It's wonderful. Makes you sound worldly. Of course, maybe you are, anyway." She paused to inhale deeply. "It's fabulous out here, isn't it?"

"It certainly is. It's one of my favorite spots."

"What do you do when you come here?" she asked. "Oh, sorry, am I being too nosy? I have a bad habit of asking too many questions."

"No, of course not. I don't mind. Today I was walking and imagining what life was like when Father Marquette and Joliet came through here."

"I don't know too much about them, except that they were explorers and the beach in Muskegon is named Pere Marquette."

Her voice seemed to caress him with every word. He wished she would never stop talking. He wanted nothing more than to remove her glasses and gaze into her eyes. He needed to see what was behind those dark lenses. 'If I keep her talking,' he thought, 'she might remove them herself.'

"You've got it right," Michael responded. "It was in the 1670s. Can you imagine traveling on Lake Michigan in a canoe? Even if you stayed close to shore, it would have been a very tedious trip. And the crossover to Wisconsin would have been brutal." He glanced over his shoulder. "If you stand here by the rails and look back, you can see nothing but dunes, trees, and grasses. Have you ever noticed?"

"No, I haven't." Emmy loved looking into his eyes, but she pulled her look away, turned around, and looked backwards. "I see what you mean. It looks so raw and natural. There's not a sign of a house. This is what they saw. I wonder what this channel looked like then."

"I'm sure there was something here, but it must have been very narrow. Maybe it started out as a small stream, or perhaps it was carved out by the Indians for access to the big lake from Muskegon Lake. It's something I'm looking into."

"Why?" Emmy wanted to continue asking questions in order to keep him talking. Her heart was racing at his nearness. He was extremely good-looking, and by the look of his long legs, he was quite tall. She wanted to stand next to him and feel his body heat and strength. His face was smooth and cleanly shaven. He smelled of a piney aftershave. She had the sudden urge to caress his cheek. She didn't remember ever having this response to Daniel.

"I'm an author – well, no, not yet, but I plan to be. Can you call yourself an author if you're not published yet?"

She studied his warm brown eyes. "You can call yourself anything you want. It's your life, so yes, you are an author. I think you'll be quite famous one day."

"Really? How would you know? We just met."

"Believe me, I have a feeling for these things." She touched his hand lightly, and pulled back when she realized she didn't know him well enough for that gesture. The contact felt good; it had seemed so natural.

"Thank you for your confidence in me." He chuckled. "I hope you're right. By the way, my name is Michael."

She sucked in her breath. "Oh, boy."

"What does that mean?"

She had not meant to say that out loud, but now that she had, she felt the need to explain. She watched Tessie as she sniffed the ground. "My father's name is Michael and my grandfather was a Michael. And there are more Mikes and Michaels in the family than I can count."

"It's a common name, I guess."

"Well," she flirted, "if we're ever to see each other again, I'll need to call you something different. I don't want a male friend with the same name as all of my family members."

"Are we seeing each other again?" He was shocked at her boldness.

She lowered her voice, tipped her head, and said, "I would love to, if you can come up with another name."

He laughed out loud. "I was always called Clay when I was young. Clayton is my middle name. I only started using Michael recently."

"Clay it is, then. I'll call you Clay. I like it."

A sapphire-colored flash passed before Michael's eyes, as he immediately remembered the gypsy's words – 'she will call you by your childhood name.'

'She's the one,' he thought. 'She's the one I am to give the bracelet to. But how and when? I can't just announce that I have some gems to return to her.' His heart was racing so fast that he was worried he might pass out.

"Is that all right?" she asked, puzzled by his expression.

"What is that?"

"Can I call you Clay?"

"Yes. Please do. I would love that, especially if it means I can see you again sometime."

She reached into the small bag hanging from her wrist, and retrieved a card. "Here's my number. Call me soon, Clay." She smiled and his world lit up. "Well, I'd better leave, now. Come, Tessie; it's time to get you home."

"Wait! I don't know your name."

She stood, then squatted down to untangled Tessie's leash. Her movements were graceful and a delight to watch. He loved the way she moved her hands. While she was busy, with her back to him, his eyes followed the line of her legs. They were long – never ending, it seemed – and perfectly shaped. Well-toned, but not too muscular. Tanned a golden color and so inviting.

She turned her head and said over her shoulder, "My name is Emmaline, but I usually go by Emmy."

"Emmy it is, then. We shall both use nicknames. When can I call you, Emmy?"

"Soon, Clay. Just don't wait too long." As she left him, so did his breath. He would not be filled with enough oxygen again until he could be with her one more time.

Chapter Ten

After another dream-filled night, Michael had no choice but to make the call. He had been putting it off, because he did not want anyone to think he was being foolish.

"Hello?"

"Hi, Ivy; it's Clay, um Michael."

"Hi, Michael. How have you been? Did you recover after the party? I'm afraid the kids got a little wild. Sorry about that."

"Oh, no problem. I enjoyed it. It felt like family."

"And you are to us. But what was that Clay thing?"

"Well, I neglected to mention when I first met you, that I usually go by Clay. It's a shortened version of my middle name."

"You mean we've been calling you the wrong name all along? Why didn't you say something?"

"It's not a problem. I had decided at that moment to try using my 'grown-up' name, but it's recently come to my attention that it doesn't fit me so well."

"Okay. Clay it is, then. I'll make sure to tell the others. So, Clay, what can I do for you?"

'Here it goes,' thought Clay.

"You might think I'm crazy, but I wonder if I could have a few moments of your time. I want to discuss your first book, well, all of them actually."

"Of course. Anything for a fellow writer. How's it going, by the way? Are you still looking for some Michigan history to write about?"

Clay chuckled. "I wasn't sure what I was going to do, I had a few irons in the fire, but I met someone yesterday who made it clear to me that Father Marquette should be my person of interest."

"That sounds like a wonderful idea. I don't have a lot of knowledge about him, but I can surely help with the writing process. When and where would you like to meet?"

"Would you prefer to come here for lunch, or go out?" asked Clay. "It's on me either way."

"I'd give anything to get back in that gorgeous house of yours. I didn't get a good look at it, with all of the commotion going on," said Ivy. She had always been fascinated by those big homes on the lake – especially this one, the one that her husband had inspected for Piper Evans.

"Do you have any plans for this afternoon? We could have lunch here on the patio."

"That sounds wonderful, but don't go to too much trouble. I know what bachelor living must be like. The cupboards are probably never fully stocked, right?" she teased.

"Actually, I have a full time cook and housekeeper now, so it's no problem at all. Shall we say 1:00?"

Ivy raised her eyebrows in surprise. "That sounds perfect. I'll be there. Is there anything I need to bring?"

"No, your pleasant company is all that I require."

"All right, I'll try my best to be pleasant, then," she chuckled. "I'll see you soon." When Ivy hung up the phone, she realized there was more to Michael Clayton Harris, the Third than she had first thought.

∞

"Ivy, I'm so glad to see you." He took her hands in his and kissed her on the cheek.

"Hi Micha – Clay, I mean." Ivy laughed, and hugged her young friend. "It's going to be tough to change your name, but I'll do it. It just might take some time."

"Yeah, sorry about that. Won't you please come in?" asked Clay, in his delightful British voice. Even though he had not lived in England for many years, he was taught proper manners by a governess and his schoolmarms at a young age. His parents continued the practice of children being seen and not heard, and teaching him the correct use of address when meeting adults. To this day, he had a difficult time calling anyone older than himself by their proper name.

Ivy noticed that Clay seemed unusually nervous. She was sure that it had to do with something more than writing his book. She was quite curious to know what he might have needed her for.

"So, how have you been, Clay?"

"You see, you did it already. It won't be difficult to make the switch, will it?"

"No," she chuckled. "And you do look more like a Clay to me, anyway. I hope the others can catch on. So, what about you? Everything okay?"

"Sure, perfectly fine." He cleared his throat, as if he was about to say something, hesitated a moment, stuttered, and instead something else altogether came out. "How about that tour now? Would you like to go through again before we eat?"

"I'd love to. By the way, have you ever met Piper Evans, the previous owner," Ivy asked, as they began to walk.

"Yes, just once, at the signing of the mortgage papers."

"And?"

"Well, um, let's just say, that woman has way too much time on her hands. I had the feeling she was coming on to me. It was quite uncomfortable."

"That's Piper, for sure."

Clay took her elbow and led Ivy into the next room as they chatted. "How exactly do you know her?"

"She's Fox's ex-wife and the boys' – Jack's and Rob's, mother."

"Oh, that's who she is! Oh my. I had no idea. I just knew that Fox had done an inspection on this house for the previous owner."

"He wasn't aware of who she was when he was first contracted for the job, but she had set the whole thing up. I had the feeling that she had purchased this house for the sole purpose of meeting him again, and maybe getting back with him, but the whole thing backfired. Anyway, old news. It's your house now, and you've done a fabulous job with it."

"Thank you, but most of the credit goes to my interior decorator."

Ivy stopped to caress a beautiful vase. "Ming? Lovely. Michael – oops, Clay, this house seems awfully grand for a single man."

"Yes, it probably is, and it does get lonely sometimes, but I'm looking to the future. I'd love to have a house full of kids like you do, and it would be a great place for them to grow up, with the lake and large yard. And there's plenty of space for each child to have their own bedroom." Michael stopped moving forward. "Here's my study, although I rarely use it. It might come in handy when there are more people living here. A good place to escape."

Ivy shook her head in silent laughter. "First, you want to fill the house with children, and then you're looking for a place to hide out. But I get it, believe me. A nice quiet place to write would be wonderful. Wow, look at this desk. The carving is exquisite. It's an antique, right, but in beautiful condition. What kind of wood?"

"Teak. It was shipped from China."

"Clay, it's none of my business, but as I look around at the house and its furnishings and your new car, I think you've been holding out on us."

"The BMW was a bit of an extravagance, but I've dreamed of owning one forever. I recently came into a bit of money, so why not?"

"Yes, why not? It's your life, after all. Enjoy it." They climbed the staircase in silence, as Ivy ran her hands over the lovely railing. At the top she looked down at the first floor entryway. "Breathtaking, just beautiful."

"Please forgive me for leading you into my bedroom, but I want to retrieve something, and then we can go back down. Feel free to roam through the other rooms, if you like."

Ivy's eyes were drawn to the balcony. "May I step out for the view?"

"Of course, be my guest."

She opened the French doors and stepped out to look at the water. Ivy couldn't believe how far out on the lake she could see. Such a different perspective from this point. A movement caught her eye, and she saw a young woman with a dog on a leash. She seemed to be coaxing it to do its duty. Ivy could barely hear her, but it sounded like she was saying something like, "Chessie, hurry up. Go pee pee." The wind and waves blocked out anything else. She turned to go back in and saw Clay at a wall safe. "Oh, sorry, I didn't mean to intrude."

"No problem. I have something to show you, but it will wait until later. Shall we go down to lunch now? The cook has it all prepared."

Ivy raised an eyebrow. Cook? Housekeeper? BMW? Mansion? There certainly is more to Clay. He's definitely been holding out on them.

Because of the windy day, Clay had decided to have their lunch in the sunroom. He pulled out a chair for Ivy, and gently pushed it in when she was seated. The glasses were already filled with sparkling ice water with a bright yellow slice of lemon hanging on the side. The glass had already begun to drip moisture on the sides. Cloth napkins had been artfully placed on their plates, while a crystal bowl of fresh cut 'Vanilla Strawberry' hydrangeas decorated the table. Clay sat opposite of Ivy so he could watch her face as he told her his story. He was just about to begin, when the cook brought out a beautiful Asian chicken salad. "Wine?" he asked.

"That would be lovely. Thank you."

As soon as the cook left the room, Clay began to say something, then stopped himself and began again. "I've brought you here under false pretenses, I suppose."

"I was beginning to suspect that," she replied.

"Yes, well, um, I have a story to tell you, but first, I need to ask about your stories."

"What do you mean?"

"About the whole Ruby and Sal thing, the necklace, you know, the rubies and diamonds."

Ivy leaned forward. She had been questioned before, and had a stock answer all set to go. "What about it?"

"It might sound crazy, but is it real? Is there such a thing as a necklace that can stir passion and bring two lovers together?"

"Let me just say, it's my story—emphasis on story -- and I never share my secrets." She winked to ease the tension.

"I can see that in order to gain your confidence, I'll need to tell you *my* story first, and if I'm correct, you might be inclined to share."

"This sounds fascinating. I love a good story, fiction or not. Go ahead. I'm a great listener."

Clay recounted his trip to London to search for his mother, and the only time she interrupted him was to ask, "And did you find her?"

"Yes, but unfortunately she wants no contact. I'll tell you all about that later, but this is really about something altogether different." Then he went on to talk about the rain and his accidental discovery of the fortuneteller's shop. "Now, here's where things get strange. And I want you to promise me that you will tell no one about this. Perhaps Fox, but only him. It can go no further."

"Of course, you can trust me. I know how to keep a secret."

"I was quite confused when I first stumbled into this shop. It seemed very familiar, yet I had never been there before. Looking back, I now realize it was so much like the one you described in your books. A beautiful young woman, dressed in colorful scarves and jewelry, was rather aggressive, sexually, shall we say, but I turned down her advances and agreed to a reading only. She wore a bracelet of sapphires and diamonds. I thought it was most likely a fake, just to make her look the part, but they sparkled more than anything I have ever seen, and when she reached out to touch my hand, sparks leapt from her wrist to mine. She said it proved it was meant for me, and right then and there, she took it off and gave it to me. I was terrified it might be stolen, but I didn't want to part with it, either. I was drawn to it, and couldn't seem to let it go. So I found a way to get it through customs and brought it home. I felt like a thief, but it was bizarre the way it did not set off any alarms. I made it home without incident, and it's been in my safe ever since."

"Is that what you took out just now?"

"Yes, and I intend to show it to you, but first I want to finish my story. Every time I take it out, there are small sparks bouncing off of it, but nothing like what it did when she first touched me. It was surreal how the gypsy woman knew my name. She called me Clay. There was no way she could have gotten it off any of my travel paperwork. I was only going by Michael then. Her words about the bracelet are what is puzzling me to this day. She said I needed to return it to 'her,' and when I asked what she meant, she said, 'You will know when the time is right. *She belongs to me, and therefore I belong to you.*'"

"That is strange, isn't it? I wonder what that meant?" commented Ivy.

"When I asked how I would know *her*, she said, 'She will call you by your childhood name.' I left there so confused. No one had called me Clay since I moved to Muskegon. My family still does, but that's just my dad and brother now, and a few aunts and uncles." Clay paused and studied Ivy's face. It seemed like she was struggling with herself about what she wanted to say. But when she did talk, Clay could tell she was still being careful with her words.

"What are you asking me, Clay? Is the story about the fortuneteller's shop real? Let me just say, I've never been to London. And my story was about Edward who found the shop in 'Maisy and Max,' and then it's mentioned again in the third book which was about Anya and Bo. Those were both flashbacks to another era, way before my time."

"So do you think I'm crazy? Because there's more."

"I'd love to hear it." Ivy held her breath until he continued with his story.

"I was taking a walk along the North Muskegon channel. I wanted to get out among people. How else am I ever to meet anyone unless I circulate? So after my walk, I sat on a bench, and a beautiful woman sat next to me. We had instant chemistry. I felt something unexplainable. We talked about so many different things, and when it was time for her to go, we realized we had never told each other our names. She introduced herself as Emmy Simmons. When I gave her my name as Michael, she said that was unacceptable, because she had too many Mikes and Michaels in her family. So I told her I also went by Clay, and she said she would call me that from now on. And then I knew. There it was. The prediction had already come true."

"But didn't you lead her that way by suggesting that as your nickname?"

"Yes, but she was the one who instigated that conversation, because she couldn't accept Michael."

"Hmm, interesting. So, the question is, are you seeing her again?"

"I'm not sure what to do. You see there's one more thing. I seem to have a strong desire for my neighbor, also, although I don't know her. I've only seen her over the fence."

"I saw her just now with a dog. But she can't be the one, Clay. She's married."

"I know, and that's what's bothering me. I was out on the balcony one night when I couldn't sleep. I had the bracelet in my hand trying to work things out. I saw her down there again, and when I looked at her in the moonlight, bright sparks flew off of the thing. I almost dropped it."

"I can see your predicament. On one hand you have a woman you've just met who wants to call you Clay, and on the other hand, there is the woman next door who creates sparks from your bracelet. Hmm. Well, Fox is acquainted with the people next door. If you'll allow me to tell him what you have just told me, I can ask what he knows about them."

"What do you think of me now, Ivy? Am I too scary to be around? Do you think I'm loony tunes?"

"Absolutely not, Clay." She laughed out loud. "If you only knew."

"So you'll still be my friend?"

"Always, Clay. You're part of the family now. After what we went through with Jack and Rob, I feel like I have adopted you all. Well, I'd better get going. I'm sure you never meant for me to hang out here all day."

"First let me show you this, so you know I'm not exaggerating." He opened the velvet bag, and dropped the bracelet into her hands.

Ivy could barely speak. Its beauty was indescribable. It was cool to the touch and glittered beyond belief. Next to her own necklace, it was the most beautiful piece of jewelry she had ever seen. All she could say was, "Oh, Clay. Oh my."

"Yes, you get it. Will you talk to Fox? I'm so confused. I want to call Emmy, but I won't if it isn't going anywhere. And I don't want to confuse the issue if the bracelet is meant for someone else. I think I believe the gypsy, so I've decided whether you think I'm a fool or not, I'm going to find the woman I'm supposed to be with."

"And you should. Everyone deserves that. To be loved by the one who was chosen for you is a special gift. And to able to return that love is even more meaningful. I'll ask Fox about your neighbors and call you right away." Ivy looked at Clay's desolate face, and pulled him in for a hug. "You'll work it out. It is meant to happen. Take care of your bracelet. It truly is special."

Once she said those words, it was all he needed to hear. Clay looked deeply into Ivy's eyes; she nodded slightly. She really did understand, even though she might never say it out loud.

Later in the day, Ivy called Clay to tell him that Fox knew the next-door neighbors well. When they had seen him working at Piper's house, they had called him over for an inspection on their home, too. They thought they had some plumbing issues that might need to be brought up to code. He said their names were Ken and Marge Thompson, and he thought they had been living there for several years. He got the impression that they had been married for a quite a while, now. This was their first home together as a couple, and at the time he worked for them, they were actively renovating and redecorating. Mrs. Thompson seemed to enjoy spending money, he said. Ivy cautioned Clay that those last words were for his ears only. Clay thanked Ivy and hung up a disappointed man. His neighbor was now officially out of the equation. He would wait a few days and maybe make contact with Emmy again. After thinking it over, he agreed with Ivy. He had probably led her to call him Clay; it had not been her idea, at all. She probably wasn't *the one*, but he could enjoy her company, nonetheless.

Chapter Eleven

Saturday was farmer's market day on Western Avenue in downtown Muskegon. It was one of Clay's favorite things to do since he had moved here. All grocery shopping was left to the cook now, but he just enjoyed being out with people. Besides there was a wide variety of things to purchase other than vegetables and fruits, but strangely enough now that he could buy anything he wanted, he found that he had suddenly become quite picky. He had seen some amazing photos of lighthouses by at least two different vendors that interested him the last time he came; he knew his decorator might not approve, but she was out of the picture now anyway. It was time to make this beautiful house his home.

Clay strolled along leisurely, picking up homemade soaps to smell, tasting free samples of fudge, and touching wooden crafts. He bought some raspberry jam, and a special roast of whole coffee beans. When a large chocolate cookie caught his eye, he asked for just one to take home. He heard a tongue click and then a sigh. Surprisingly, when he turned to his right, he saw Emmy. "Are you irritated with me?" he asked with a grin.

"Oh, Clay, it's you. I was just about to get that cookie. They're the best."

"Here, take it. I'll get a macadamia nut; my treat."

"Thank you, you're such a gentleman," she said, as she smiled sweetly. She was dressed the same as she had been at the channel when he first met her – large hat and big sunglasses, but she wore a long sundress of bright summer colors. He only recognized her because of her earrings which were the same she was wearing before. The silver dangling chains with tiny stars at the end moved when she talked and gestured. The sapphires caught his eye as they sparkled in the sun. Sapphires? Could it be? They mesmerized him; he took a step closer, but she moved back, keeping her personal space between them blocked out.

"Will you walk with me?" he asked tentatively.

"I'd like that. I wasn't sure if I would ever see you again. You didn't call."

"I thought you might call *me*," he said with a chuckle. "Where is it written that it's the man's job?"

"It's written in my book of rules. I like it that way. I'm old-fashioned, I guess." She smiled and his heart melted.

"Sorry, I've been a bit confused about things lately."

"Me, too, actually."

"You have? About what?"

"That's a little too much for you to know right now."

"Okay, sorry. I didn't mean to pry."

The wind off the lake moved gently over them. He still had not seen her hair and eyes. How he wished the breeze would blow that hat off her head, but when it moved a little, she tied it down with a leather thong and sliding bead which was attached to the hat and had been hanging loosely at her chin.

"Look, Clay, I don't want to lead you on. I shouldn't have been so forward at the channel. I'm sort of seeing someone – well, not sort of. I am. We've been together a long time."

"Oh, I see. But why did you give me your number, then?"

"I was upset with him at the time. I thought it was time to call it off, but I just can't. We have too much history between us."

"I can't say I'm not disappointed. I thought we had a lot in common. I really enjoy talking to you."

"I like talking to you, too. But I think we should just call ourselves friends. Acquaintances, really."

"Sure, sure, I get it. Okay, want to give me my cookie back now?" He laughed to try to show that he was not hurt. They had only met one time before. He shouldn't expect anything from her, but being this near to her, he found himself wanting to pull her to him and kiss her beautiful mouth right then and there. He could feel his heart pounding through his chest. Clay pulled his own sunglasses from his pocket and put them on to cover a few tears that had sprung to his eyes. He hoped she had not seen the emotion he was trying to conceal.

She touched his hand. "Sorry, Clay. Maybe I'll see you again sometime."

He gave a little wave as she walked out of his life.

∞

Later that evening, after he had returned to the the house, Clay was even more puzzled than before. He had totally been misreading the signs that he thought Emmy was giving. Apparently, she had just wanted to be friends. Clay wondered what was wrong with him. Ever since his previous girlfriend had broken up with him, he had not been able to find any companionship. He had lost his confidence.

Clay climbed his stairs to take a shower. Maybe he could clear his head when the hot water was beating on his body. As he washed his hair, he decided his problems were all due to that stupid bracelet. The idea of its capabilities had put fanciful ideas into his thoughts. Thinking there was a perfect girl out there who was waiting just for him – someone who had been chosen by the universe to be his one and only -- was crazy! He had to stop this.

He stepped outside of the shower and wrapped a thick towel around his waist. His broad chest was still damp, his chest hair curled in tight ringlets, and his wet hair was plastered to his head. Neglecting to wipe himself down, Clay left a trail of dripping water on the carpet as he walked to his nightstand. He had forgotten to put the bracelet back in the safe after Ivy was here. That in itself showed how he had been walking around in a daze. Even if the thing wasn't magical, it must be worth a lot of money. He picked it up and a few sparks shot out of it again. Ridiculous! There wasn't even a woman around. He carried it with him as he went to his small bar to pour himself a drink. He'd had the bar installed in case he ever did have any female companionship up here, but that plan looked pretty bleak. Right now, though, the bourbon could settle his nerves at least. Walking out to the balcony, with the bracelet in his hand, he sat on one of the thickly cushioned chairs. The blue and white upholstery, meant to mimic the colors of the lake, instead, picked up the same shades as the bracelet. He took a small sip and then placed his drink and the jewels on the small table beside him. He was staring at the water, contemplating his life, when a few seconds later, he heard some conversation next door.

He knew it was wrong, because they never seemed to notice him up here, but he stood up to watch, totally forgetting he was still clad in only a towel. There she was, the other woman who haunted his dreams. She was with the same man again who he now assumed was her husband. She was wearing a ruby red dress, which conformed tightly to her shape, tucked in at the waist, and then flared over her hips; the loose skirt moved gently with the breeze. The top of the dress was a halter top; on the backside it cascaded to a deep V, exposing a bare back. Her high heels accented her long legs and trim ankles, causing Clay to think that she had probably been to a formal event. Her dark hair was piled thick and high on top of her head. She carried out a tray of food, as the man followed behind with some drinks; it looked like glasses of red wine. If Clay had turned around, he would have seen some sparks jumping from the bracelet on his table, but he was too absorbed in what was going on down there. When they placed their trays on the table, the man wrapped his arms around her and pulled her in close. Clay could almost feel her warm skin on his; he wondered if she felt like velvet. Then the man began to kiss her deeply as he released her hair from its coil on top. It fell like a waterfall had cascaded to her waist, ending at the V of the dress near her deliciously rounded bottom. The man wound his fingers through the dark strands, and Clay heard a passionate moan from him. 'Why does she never turn my way?' Clay wondered. Married or not, he just had to see what she looked like. 'Marge' pulled back a bit, and flipped her hair to one side until it settled over her shoulder. She laughed at something he said. 'Her husband, Ken,' came back for more as he worked his fingers at her neck under her hair and then he untied the straps to the top of the dress, letting one side fall. Clay knew it was time to look away, but he just could not do it. He seemed to be frozen to the spot. What he saw next surprised him. When her husband reached for his prize, Clay clearly heard her say, "Stop." Then she pushed him away. Why would a woman react that way to her husband? Had they recently had a fight? He could not hear anything specific, but there were angry words, coming from both sides. The next thing he knew, the man stormed into the house; then he heard a car start and tires squeal as the car roared down the street.

The woman, 'Marge,' picked up the front of her top and held it closely to her body as she slowly walked back into the house. Her head hung forward, creating a curtain of hair which blocked out her face. Clay stayed on the patio for a while sipping his drink, pondering over what he had just seen. Once again he was ashamed of himself for watching, but what was a man to do? It was like a movie playing out before him, and all he could think about was why had she not turned around? Because now, besides wondering about her face, he had something else to dream about. Tonight in his dreams he would be the man who freed what was under the red halter top, and she would not argue with him. She would willingly and eagerly consent.

∞

Two days later, when Emmy opened the door, Daniel was standing there with a sheepish grin holding a bouquet of flowers. "Am I forgiven?"

She studied his little boy grin for a second. She had always had a soft spot for him. "Of course you are. We've been friends for too long to let a little misunderstanding keep us apart. Come in, silly." She took the flowers, pulled him in for a quick kiss, and went searching for a vase.

"Hey, is that all I get?"

Emmy glanced over her shoulder while she searched in the cupboard for the right size vase. "Isn't that what got you into trouble in the first place?"

"You mean that I wanted more from you? Come on, Em, we've always been close, since we were kids. You know we've experimented on more than one occasion. A lot, actually. I want more than being 'friends with benefits' now. I love you."

"I know. I just didn't feel like it then, and you didn't want to take no for an answer. Besides we were outside, for Pete's sake."

Daniel came up behind her and wrapped his arms around her waist. He nibbled her ear because he knew she loved it, but she gently pushed him away like a mother would a child. He was puzzled. Something had changed. "What is it? What's wrong?"

"Nothing. I, uh, I've been thinking about us a lot lately."

"What about us?" he asked, afraid to hear the answer.

"Well, it's just that we've been together for so long. We've never been with anyone else – well, I never have." She stopped talking long enough to catch the guilty look on his face. "Oh, so you have been with other women. Well, that's news to me."

"Sorry, but it's a guy thing, you know?"

"No, I don't know. I didn't know. I'm disappointed in a way, but doesn't that tell you something? You're playing around, and I'm questioning our relationship. I think our little high school boyfriend/girlfriend thing has run its course."

"But, Emmy, what will I do without you in my life? Are you saying you want to call it quits altogether? I don't know if I can bear that."

"Danny, we'll always be friends. But I don't think we were meant to be long-term lovers. We don't really have anything in common."

"We do love to do *one* thing together." He gave her a sexy smile.

"See, that's what I mean. I don't want to be your booty call. I'm ready for something else. I want a man who can be my partner in life, and the father to my children. I'm not sure you're ever going to settle down."

"But, Em – I'll be lost without you."

"I don't think so. Go play the field. Give it a try, maybe you'll find your one true love; but I know one thing for sure. It's not me."

Daniel truly did look crestfallen. She had not anticipated that. She raised herself up on her toes and kissed him lightly on the cheek. "Thanks for the flowers. It was sweet."

"Yes, it was, wasn't it?" His demeanor change instantly. He flashed her a cocky grin, and then without warning, he pulled her in close for a long passionate kiss. "One for the road. If you're sure this is truly a breakup, I'll be leaving now. But never forget that I'll always be there for you, now and forever. You're one of a kind, Emmy. A true gem. You deserve the best. Don't settle for anything less."

"Thanks for saying that, my sweet Danny. We'll see each other again soon. I promise. But friends only, okay?"

"Sure, okay." And with one last lingering look, he turned and walked out, leaving her shaken. She had not thought that would be so hard.

As Daniel closed the door behind him, his shoulders slumped and his head fell forward. He had just lost his best friend and lover. The others girls had been just for fun, and meant nothing, but he had always loved Emmy. That's what he told himself, anyway, as he walked slowly to his car.

Chapter Twelve

Rob, Jack, and Paul rang the doorbell at the mansion on the lake.

"I feel a little intimidated every time we come here," said Jack. "Who knew Michael – Clay had this kind of money?"

"I sure didn't. But he's being very generous with his boat, so I'll take it," laughed Rob.

"Well, I for one, could never afford to own a boat like his. I can't wait to get out on the big water and do some fishing," added Paul.

The door was opened by the housekeeper. "Please come in. Mr. Harris will be right down. He said you are to make yourself at home. He sends his apologies, but he received an unexpected phone call. Can I get you anything to drink?"

"Sure," they all responded.

"Whatever you have," answered Jack. "We shouldn't drink alcohol if we're going on the boat, so anything else will do."

"Iced tea?" she asked.

"Great," said the twins in unison.

"You guys are too funny," said Paul.

"I'll never get used to the fact that you were twins and we never knew it. What a day that was."

"At Ivy and Dad's party? It sure was," said Jack. "It was one of the best days of my life."

"I remember -- "

"Sorry, guys," called Clay. "I got a call from overseas. I felt I had to take it."

"Business?" asked Paul, curiously. None of the guys had ever been informed about Clay's lottery winnings, and they were always curious to know where the money had come from. At this point they could only assume he had inherited a bundle, since he didn't have a job.

"Yes, uh, it was from someone I hired in London. It seems that he has heard once again from my mother."

"Your biological mother?" asked Rob. "I guess I wasn't aware that you had found her."

"Yes, I did. They were able to locate her, and they made contact when I was in London."

"That's great. Tell us all about it!" said Jack, always interested in someone else's birth parents.

"There's not much to tell. She wasn't ready to meet me when I was there. I can understand that, considering the circumstances – she was raped, you know. But it's been a while now, 26 years in fact. Mr. Blythe just called to say he had once again reached out to her, and she's adamant that she doesn't want her family to know about me. So I guess that's a dead end."

"So sorry, man," said Paul, adding a manly slap on the back.

"No problem. I was expecting it. Besides, it's not like I didn't have a good upbringing. I had a great mother. I couldn't have asked for more. I miss her every day. She was always so wise and kind and giving. Everyone loved her."

"Well, at least you know your birth mother's name, and maybe you can get some heritage information or medical information through your investigator. That was the main thing for us, when we had Jackson," added Paul, in a comforting tone.

"You're right. I hadn't thought that far into the future. I might have children someday, and it would be important then, wouldn't it? I'll see if he can get anything else out of her, but I doubt it."

"Too bad, pal," said Jack. Always the life of the party, he changed the tone of his voice and with a big grin, he said, "Hey, are we ever going fishing?"

By circumventing the subject, everyone's mood lightened up. All of a sudden the men were joking about who would catch the biggest fish, and wagers were made. As they stepped outside, their gasps were audible.

"What's that?"

"Holy cow, man."

"Who does that belong to?"

"Whoa, one at a time," laughed Clay. This is when he loved having money – it was meant to have a good time with his buddies. Moored farther out, beyond the end of the dock, in deeper water, was a brand new boat, one they had not seen before.

"Is that yours?" said Rob, in awe.

"Is it new?" asked Jack.

Clay grinned, proud of his new purchase. "Yup, it was just delivered yesterday. It's a Robalo R317. – 31 foot. Top of the line. It's got everything we'll need. The smaller boat is good for speed and towing water skiers, but this one will respond better in the deep water."

"Well, the other one is great, but this is -- wow," said Rob. "Just wow. She's a beaut. And the name? Where did you come up with that?"

"I'm not sure," lied Clay, looking at the *Sapphire C* painted on the side and back of the boat. "It just came to me. I liked sapphire for the blue of the sky and water, and of course the initial C stands for Clay, but it's also a pun for sea. It works, don't you think?"

"I think we're darned lucky to have you for a friend," joked Paul.

"Okay, boys. Load up the dingy. We need to motor out, anchor it, and climb aboard. Then we can get out of here," he called.

∞

Emmy was on her terrace with Tessie. She had planned to get some sun as soon as the little thing finished up her business. Then Tessie would have to go back inside, since it was too hot out here for her. Already dressed in her orange bikini, sunglasses, and a large woven hat, she hoped not to be interrupted until she was done reading. It was supposed to be hot and humid all afternoon, followed by heavy rains later, so she wanted to be outside in the morning, before the weather changed. She was in the middle of an Ivy Morton book and was looking forward to reading the next chapter. She heard the raucous male voices from next door, but for the most part she ignored them. There was always something going on at the lake, and voices carried so much over the water, that she had learned to block them out.

But what she did hear was "Hey, man, who's that? Oowee, she's something else."

Then she heard someone mumble something, and a "Hey, you're married."

"A guy can look, can't he?" and then more laughter.

"How about you? You're single. Get over there and get it done." Then there were some whistles and catcalls.

"Hey, I have to live here. Behave."

Emmy had heard it all before. It was part of being a beautiful woman. 'Men! They never think we notice,' thought Emmy. The boat's motor roared to life as it began its trip out to the big lake, leaving a bunch of hoots and hollers behind to float over the waves. "So childish," she said out loud to Tessie. "You get it; right, Miss Cheng? Yup, I knew you would." She hooked up the little dog to the yard chain, then took off her hat, removed her glasses, and let her hair fall loose. It was only a few short months until her sister returned. She planned to make the most of living the good life.

$$\infty$$

The men had had a very successful fishing day, but after several hours out, the sky began to darken, and rather than wait for it to threaten them any further, they decided to call it a day. When Clay pulled the boat in, he couldn't help but look at his neighbor's yard, and he was somewhat disappointed to see that it was empty. Of course, she would have gone in. He couldn't expect her stay out there the whole time they were out on the water. Maybe someday he would have a chance to talk to her; then he chided himself on coveting his neighbor's wife. Still a man could dream, couldn't he? What was the harm in having fantasies in the night? No one would ever know.

After the guys left, Clay had a quiet supper by himself, as he usually did. It had been so good to spend some time with his buddies, but here he was, alone again. They each had someone to go home to, to talk about the day's events, and to make love with at night. Why was love so elusive for him? He decided to go upstairs to watch some TV in his room. The clouds were rolling in now and the sky was almost black even though it was only 7:00. He stepped out on the balcony to watch the storm move in from Lake Michigan. It looked like it was going to be fierce. He was glad all of the guys had made it home in time.

Just as Clay turned to go back into the house, the rain let loose. He saw her running out to lower the sun umbrella before the wind turned it inside out. Her hair was whipping about her face, and was soon plastered to it. She grabbed the chair cushions and threw them inside, but just then the little dog ran out.

"No, Tessie! Come back here."

A crack of lightening followed by a loud boom of thunder scared the poor thing, and she ran, with her tail between her legs, under the hedge fence. He watched as 'Marge' ran out, trying to find her dog in the downpour. As Clay continued to watch, he saw that the dog had come through the hedge and was now on his side. He ran downstairs, and out the door in his bare feet. He could hear 'Marge' shrieking on the other side in a panic for the dog. He called 'Chessie, here Chessie' and she came right to him, shivering in fear at the next crack of lightening.

"Here," he yelled, "over here. I've got her."

"I'm going to the end of the hedge," she yelled.

Clay ran down to meet her, but she came around the end before he got there, meeting him on his side of the yard. She was soaked to the skin. She held her head down to avoid the beating rain; her hair was plastered to her back and cheeks. She reached out for her dog. "You naughty, girl," she chided, pulling the shaking puppy to her. Her voice recalled warm feelings all the way through him. She looked up to say thank you, froze for a moment, and finally said in shock, "Clay?"

Chapter Thirteen

Clay was so stunned he couldn't speak. It was Emmy, or he thought it was, since he had never seen her eyes. But she was really Marge, wasn't she? Suddenly another lightning strike on the water came too close and a deafening thunder immediately followed. 'Chessie' almost jumped out of her arms again, so he took hold of Marge/Emmy's arm and pulled her to his house.

"Quick," he yelled over Mother Nature's racket, "let's get inside."

As they ran toward the door, one electrical hit after another followed right behind them, seeming to push them toward the house. They got in just before another large boomer caused 'Chessie' to jump from Marge/Emmy's arms.

"Tessie, you're all wet. Come here." The little ball of drenched fur shook herself off vigorously before retreating under a chair. Droplets of rain water were scattered everywhere.

"Tessie, is it? I thought you were saying Chessie, with a C H. I guess she doesn't care about her name, because she came to me, anyway. Good thing, right? You're both shivering. Let me get you some towels."

Clay ran to the closest bathroom and grabbed one bath towel for Tessie and two large bath sheets for themselves, while Emmy got down on her knees and retrieved Tessie.

"Here, you can dry her off on this. And this one's for you."

"Thank you so much. You're a lifesaver."

He couldn't believe she was actually in his house. Her hair was flattened to her head and was dripping down her back. "Oh, let me get one more for your hair."

147

When he returned he went straight to the fireplace and stoked up a fire. When renovating, he had had the option of a gas fire with a clicker to start it, or the real thing. He had insisted on keeping the fireplace original, which meant always having wood on hand, but to this date he had not had to use the fireplace, so the wood supply was plentiful. Clay stacked the wood over the starter pieces, then put the long match underneath it all. It wasn't long before the fire was warming up the room, and it was none too soon, because with one more crack and boom, which caused all three to jump, the lights went out. The firelight's reflection allowed Clay to find his way to the cupboard that held the candles, and he quietly began the job of lighting them and strategically placing them around. As he did so, he glanced at the woman who was in his house with her dog. She seemed totally engrossed in drying and warming the animal. She cooed and talked softly to calm Tessie down, but no words were spoken between the two of them. When he was finished, he started to tend to himself. Clay rubbed his head first with the towel, then wrapped himself up with the thick bath sheet.

When she finally looked up and spoke, Clay thought his heart would go through his chest. She was here, in his living room. Her shirt was matted to her chest. He could see her lovely shape, but she held the dog in front of her preventing the view of what he really wanted to see. He noticed that she was shivering, so he said, "Come, sit here. It's closer to the fire."

"Thank you. I'm freezing."

"If you'll trust me with the dog, you can go into the guest bathroom on the second floor. There's a new robe and slippers there. It's been waiting for my first guest. Just up the stairs, then it's the second bedroom on the right."

She ducked her head, shyly. "Thank you, that's so kind."

"Emmy?"

"Yes?"

"We'll need to talk when you come back down."

"Yes, we will. I won't be long."

"Take a candle with you, and be careful on the steps."

As Clay took Tessie from her, their eyes met, but she pulled her gaze away. The color of her irises were a beautiful hazel mixture of brown and green. Clay's heart skipped a beat. As she stood to walk away, she turned and smiled slightly. She looked deeply at him for a moment, before climbing the stairs. Even though the situation was uncomfortable, he felt as though she was flirting with him once again, and she had returned back to the Emmy he had first met. But she was married. What was her game, he wondered. He sat closer to the fire, so the little bundle in his arms could warm up, but at this point he thought her shivers were more from the noise of the storm.

When Emmy came back down, she was a vision, a glorious vision. Carefully stepping on the stairs while holding the candle, she was as graceful as a slow motion movie. She wore the long white terry robe, tied loosely at the waist, but it had opened slightly at her chest and had parted just above the knee as she moved, exposing bare legs and feet. She wore nothing underneath as far as he could see, and he wondered if she had removed everything. Was she naked? His breath caught and his heart began to beat rapidly. With her hair bound up turban-style, with a towel wrapped high on her head, she seemed to him to be as regal as a queen. She was truly magnificent. He imagined her wearing the bracelet. It would sparkle in the firelight in contrast to the white terrycloth. Would it send sparks around her wrist? Was she the one? If so, why was she already married?

Emmy felt Clay's eyes on her as she descended the stairs. She started to say something, but changed her mind. Once she was seated, she simply asked, "How's Tessie?"

"She's settling in just fine. I got her a nice soft cushion to lie on by the fire."

She laughed, and it sounded like music to his ears. "You're spoiling her."

"I have a feeling she's already spoiled."

"You're right about that!" she chuckled.

"Are you warm enough? How about a hot toddy?"

"That sounds delicious."

Clay began to get up and then remembered they had no power. "Oops, no electricity, and I have an electric stove. That means no microwave, either. I guess a hot toddy is out. Just whiskey and water, or how about ginger ale?"

"A whiskey and ginger sounds great."

"I'll have one too, then." He busied himself with the drinks while he tried to figure out what was happening. He decided the best approach was to straight out ask what he wanted to know.

She was on the floor next to Tessie, bent forward, and singing a lullaby. The glow of the firelight behind her created an image that would be etched in his brain for the rest of his life.

"Here you go. Now, take a few sips, and then I have some questions."

"I'm sure you do."

After a quiet pause, she said, "Go ahead. What do you want to know?"

"How was it that I didn't know you were my neighbor?"

"How was it that I didn't know you were mine?" she countered.

"I'm not sure. I guess it was the hedge, but I have seen you from up above --

"What?" She sat up and looked right at him. "You've been watching me?"

He watched her face, as she quickly went through the times she had sunbathed in next to nothing, and the times she and her husband were outside making love, or about to.

"To be clear, I have not been watching you on purpose. It wasn't like I was a stalker or peeping Tom or anything. It's just that sometimes, when I was on my balcony, you were down there. And I couldn't help but see you."

She immediately felt like her privacy had been violated. "What exactly did you see?" she asked angrily.

"I uh, I um," Clay stuttered. "Well, I'll just say it. I watched you kissing your husband. I watched him attempting to remove your clothing and make love to you, and I watched you dancing in the moonlight in your filmy robe. Is that enough?"

"How dare you!"

Emmy stood up to leave, and as she did so, her robe fell open at the top just enough for Clay to see everything he had been dreaming about.

She saw where his eyes were looking, and she clutched her top to body. "Men!"

"Sorry, so sorry, but in my defense, you did flash me. And, yes, I am a healthy male. I'll look if given the opportunity," he smiled an apology. "It's in my genes. Please sit. The storm is still wicked. I don't think you want to walk across the wet grass and risk getting electrocuted." Anything to keep her here a little longer.

"You're probably right. I'm stuck here, I guess." She sat down and took another drink of her whiskey. Tessie was curled up on the pillow, looking like a ball of fluff. Her head was on her paws, but her eyes watched them closely. Emmy reached out and stroked her small brow, and Tessie's eyes closed. She was exhausted after her ordeal. "For the record, that was not my husband you saw. That was Danny, Daniel Luca, my boyfriend. Well, it *was* my boyfriend. We recently broke up."

He almost spit out his drink. She had a lover, and she was admitting to it? Then who was her husband, because the man he had seen was not Ken, apparently. He really didn't know this woman at all.

"So then my question to you is, why did you tell me your name is Emmy? Is the name Emmy just an alter ego? Were you planning on having another affair and using me to satisfy your urges?"

"What?" she sputtered. "I can't believe your audacity. My name *is* Emmy. What are you insinuating?" she sputtered in anger.

"You know what I mean. You see a single man of means next door and you seek him out, looking for your next conquest?" Clay was sure now that she somehow knew about his winnings. "You said your nickname is Emmy, but if that's true, what is your full name, then?"

"Emmaline Regina Simmons, just as I told you before." She watched as shock slowly spread over his face.

"What? Well -- who is Marge? You know, Marge and Ken Thompson, the people who own the house next door?"

Her face went from confusion to sorting things out, then the laughter erupted. Laughter from deep within. Laughter that brought tears to her eyes and made her gasp for breath. All the while he watched on, totally lost with what was happening.

"For the love of God, tell me what you're laughing at?"

"You thought -- you were watching -- and oh my, an affair – and oh boy, wait till Marge..."

She was holding onto her side, bent over double. Taking a deep breath, she wiped her eyes. Emmy looked up at his poor confused face and almost started in again, but she managed to get herself under control. "I'm Marge's sister. Ken is my brother-in-law. They're on a four-month cruise, so I'm housesitting and taking care of Tessie."

As everything she said began to sink in, Clay's face changed several different shades. First pink with humiliation, then deep red with embarrassment, and then white with shock when he reviewed all of the incorrect ideas he had had. At last his proper color returned when he realized she *was* Emmy. No husband, no more boyfriend, just his Emmy. He had been dreaming about, and yes, lusting after, the same woman, not two different ones. And no sooner than those thoughts ran through his head, the thunder and lightning died down, only to remain distant flashes and rumbles as the storm moved on, leaving only a hard pelting rain behind.

Clay grinned and put out his hand. "Can we start again? Nice to meet you, Emmaline Regina Simmons. My name is Michael Clayton Harris the Third, but you can call me Clay." When she took his hand, everything felt right with the world.

Chapter Fourteen

The steady rain continued throughout the night, and with the lack of electricity, Emmy and Clay had no choice but to stay together near the fire.

"I'm so glad Tessie led me to you," said Emmy. "I don't know what I would have done if I had to stay in that big old house all by myself in the dark. I never asked Marge where she kept the candles and flashlights."

Clay reached out for her hand. "I'm glad she brought you to me, too. I really wanted to see you again, but at the farmer's market you said that you were taken."

The two had moved closer to the fire and were now seated on the floor next to Tessie, who seemed perfectly content just to be in their presence. Emmy pushed some still damp hair behind her ear. "I was taken at the time I saw you that day. I was having trouble with my relationship with Daniel because I had feelings for you. I thought it was best if we called it quits before we got started. I didn't want to hurt Danny."

"But you didn't mind hurting me?" asked Clay, softly.

Emmy studied him a moment. "I didn't really know you very well, and I still don't."

"Then why did you end it with him?"

"Because I was hoping I would run into you again someday, maybe at the farmer's market or at the pier. I was hoping you would give me another chance. It felt like there was something worth exploring between us."

"I felt it from the moment I first laid eyes on you — even though I couldn't see your eyes," he laughed. The hair she had just tucked behind her ears fell forward again. In a brave move, he reached out and put it back in place. Clay had read somewhere that there were certain steps to courtship and the reason why so many new couples go wrong is that they do not take those steps in proper order. They go straight to the bed and then wonder where all of the romance went. First, two new people should make eye contact – check. Next, they might touch hands or one will touch the other's arm – check. Hair for a woman is very personal, so the next step will only be taken if the male suspects acceptance – he will cautiously touch her hair and maybe make a comment about it. Clay leaned a bit closer. She didn't pull back. "Do you mind? I have been longing to do this all evening."

"What?" she asked, breathlessly.

"Your hair. You always had it tucked under a hat whenever I saw you, but the woman on the patio let it hang down her back. I was very attracted to that hair. It made her so mysterious, but I couldn't see that woman's face, or I would have recognized you. No, I take that back. Those darned huge glasses you wore always blocked out your face. I'm so happy I can finally look into your eyes." Clay took in a deep breath and shuddered. Emotions he had never felt before were coursing through his veins.

Emmy placed her hand over his which hovered near her ear, and then he moved his palm to her cheek — step four in courtship was face. With her touch, he knew exactly what he wanted to do next. Step five. He slowly leaned forward as she moved toward him in the age old dance of lovers. When his lips touched hers, it felt like he was touching a soft pillow in Heaven. He could truly say he had never felt any other lips as soft as Emmy's. He longed to find out if the rest of her body was the same.

Emmy had never felt a kiss like that in all of her life. It was soft and gentle, but not like the childish first kiss she had had at the age of thirteen. And it was nothing like Danny's kisses. He had been demanding lately, a little rough, but not really passionate. It was as if he felt he owned her. She had given him far too much leeway over the years, and even though they had been intimate, she had never felt the thrill she was hoping for.

She had always dreamed of goosebumps, curling toes, and flashing lights, when she met the man she would spend the rest of her life with. She could see now that Daniel had never been *the* one. And maybe Clay wasn't either, but there was something to be said about taking it slow and easy. Their kiss was absolutely luscious and quite sensual. She planned to let the sexual tension build this time, instead of running into it full force.

Clay pulled back to see if she would give him another signal to move forward, but she, too, pulled back. She smiled shyly, and said, "Oh, my." Then she thought, 'Tessie, what have you started?'

To break a little of the tension and give himself some space to breathe, Clay said, "Let me refresh our drinks. The fridge is still keeping things cold. Would you care for the same or perhaps some wine instead?"

"Yes, I'd love wine."

"White or red?"

"White."

"Somehow I knew that."

"What do you mean?" Emmy asked.

Clay wondered if he should say it, but he forged ahead anyway. "Women with your figure are usually watching calories. White wine has fewer. Am I right?"

"Actually, not true. I never watch calories. I have good genes, I guess. I just happen to prefer white."

"Good to know. I'll make sure I stock up on white." He carried her glass to her, and their hands touched again when he passed it by its stem over Tessie's head. "So tell me about yourself."

Emmy took a sip and looked up through eyelashes. She always hated this part. Talking about herself never came easily. There were some things she always needed to hide, and it was difficult not to say too much.

"Well, there's really not much to tell. I'm a school teacher, but I lost my job and so now I'm at my sister's mercy. I'm on the list to substitute in the fall, so at least I'll have an income, but it won't be enough to live on."

"How does that make you feel? Do you like living there?"

"Oh, it's fine now. She's not there, but when she comes home, life gets a little more complicated. She can be very demanding. There are family dynamics that have always made things difficult between us."

Clay watched her beautiful dark eyes. He wondered what ancestry she had. Her hair, eyes, and warm skin tone and coloring suggested something like Italian or Spanish – European at any rate, maybe Eastern European. "I can certainly understand that," he answered. "You see, I'm adopted. And so is my brother, but we don't have the same biological parents. Even though we had great adopted parents, we never really bonded with each other. We're just different, I guess. We tolerate each other, shall we say."

"So we have difficult siblings in common. What else is there?" questioned Emmy, as she watched his index finger trace the rim of the glass. His fingers were long but not effeminate. His hands were strong without callouses. It was obvious he was not used to manual labor. They were hands made for making love. She shivered and let her eyes roam up his forearms. She loved that curve of flesh that all men had right before the elbow. Clay's sleeves started there, at the elbow;

otherwise she would have loved looking at his biceps. She imagined they were well-toned, but not bulging with muscles. They would be strong arms, arms made for pleasing a woman. A thrill of anticipation ran through her. She shook her head to stop any further fantasy.

"Are you cold?"

"Oh, no. Sorry. I was just thinking of something. I --

The lights flickered off and on two times and then finally stayed on for good. "Wonderful. The power is back on," she said, the pitch of her voice denying her enthusiasm.

"Yes, they are, aren't they?" Clay, too, was disappointed. Now, she would leave him, and his life would be empty once again. He offered her a hand as she got up, then he pulled her toward him and placed his arms around her waist. "Can I see you again – now that there is no one standing in our way?"

Emmy was aware that her robe was pulling apart as they stood close together. She wanted nothing more, at that moment, than to open it the rest of the way. She would love to give him full access, but she would not do it this time. "Yes," she said breathlessly. "I'd love to see you again."

Clay kissed her again, but this time with a little more pressure than he had used before. He could feel her body mold to his, as she wound her arms around his neck. When a small moan escaped her, he knew he had to separate from her, or he could ruin everything. "I'll call you later."

"Clay?" she whispered, in between small kisses.

"Hmm?"

"I need to go change back into my clothes. They're upstairs."

"Oh, yes, yes, you do. Look, your clothes might still be wet, so you can wear the robe home." He glanced down, but she was too quick and had already tightly tied the robe around her waist.

"Okay, thanks, I'll just go up and grabbed my things, then." As she went upstairs, Tessie followed her, bouncing up the steps with agility Clay would never have dreamed she possessed, her short legs causing her chest to drag on the stairs. He laughed at the sight.

When she was out of view, he felt a hole in his heart – a hole that needed to be filled, or he would surely die.

Chapter Fifteen

The sun was streaming through Emmy's bedroom window. She was having wonderful dreams and had no desire to get out of bed, but Tessie was jumping at her. The dear little thing rarely barked, so when she jumped it was serious business. Emmy sat up and stretched before getting up and sliding her feet into her slippers. Tessie was in a big hurry. She raced all the way down the stairs and was waiting for Emmy at the door. It was then that she remembered that Tessie had not gone out before they went to bed because it was still drizzling and she hated to get wet. And since she had come home in the wee hours of the night, it had not been too appealing for Emmy to stand outside in the dark while Tessie did her business. Emmy hooked up her harness and let her leash stretch out into the yard while she stayed inside the door. Emmy was never one to sleep in much clothing; she had spent last night in nothing but her tee shirt. So standing inside the door was imperative. She was not about to give any more fisherman something to talk about.

"Hurry up, Tess. I'm getting cold. Go on, you can do it." And finally she had. Tessie raced back into the house, looking for a treat – a reward for performing what she would have done anyway -- and left little wet paw prints on the tiles. Then Tessie ran to a toy and raced around the house, throwing it over her back and catching it, as if to say if no one will play with me, then I'll play by myself. Emmy laughed out loud at the little clown.

For the first time in a very long time, laughter came easily and it felt good. Emmy's dreams, during what was the rest of the night, had been of the handsome man next door, and now that she was home alone, she wondered why she had not consented to more, when she knew that's what they both wanted.

Taking a cup of hot tea to the sofa by the picture window facing the water, she mulled over the events of the evening. Emmy felt like she had a much better idea now of who the man named Clay was. They had spent their hours in the candlelit room telling each other about their childhood and families. But Emmy had withheld the one thing that always chased men away. It was something they could never understand, and quite frankly, scared them. It was her talent for seeing through lies, and her ability to see the future.

Over the years, Emmy had learned how to use this gift to her advantage. But she had to admit that sometimes she had gotten it wrong, so she was always careful as to how she released her information to others. This time she was hoping to use her ability for herself, so she had brought something home from the mansion next door. Tucked into the robe pocket was a necktie Clay had left tossed on his bed. She had tiptoed into his room when she was upstairs changing her clothes, because she had wanted something personal that he owned. It helped her to 'see' things. Strangely, when she was in his room, she saw a spark coming from behind a picture on the wall. She wanted to tell Clay about it, in case there was an electrical short, but then she would have to admit to being in his room. She had watched the area for a moment and when she saw that it had just been that single spark, after which there was nothing, she decided it must have been her imagination. But now, as she sat here looking out at the fog rolling in toward the shore, she knew that spark must have been meant for her. With Clay's tie wound around her hands, her vision saw many sparks, like a child's 4th of July sparkler. They were shooting out little stars in all directions, and something blue and glittery was present, too. She saw herself dancing with Clay. She was safe in his arms. He held her close and whispered in her ear. He made her feel warm and happy, but immediately following that scene, she felt chilled to the bone. She shivered as the vision she had seen many times before descended upon her once again. It was dark; it was void of life; it was death. For the first time she had seen how she would leave this Earth.

This was the secret she had never shared with anyone, and now she could see that it was somehow connected to Clay. She had never been given enough of the vision to know how she was to die and exactly when, but she knew it would happen when she was still a young woman. It had been her biggest dilemma, because knowing this had changed her view of life and how she should live it. If she had her way, she would love to throw caution to the wind and just live with no restrictions or worries about social etiquette. She wanted to be a free spirit; she wanted to make love outdoors under the stars; she wanted to shed her clothing and be naked for the rest of her life; she wanted to drink lots of wine, until it carried her senses away and she no longer worried about the consequences; she wanted to fall in love so deeply with a man that when she died, he would die with her. But if she were to throw caution to the wind like that, she would hurt others.

How could she ever ask a man to love her, knowing she would leave him soon? Emmy wondered if the best course was just to take love in small doses, so she could feel enough to satisfy her own soul, but not hurt the one she was with, like she had with Danny. Was that possible? She had to tread carefully with Clay; they were just at the beginning of a relationship. She could easily see herself falling in love with him. He was handsome, educated, intelligent, funny, and apparently very wealthy. But of course, money meant nothing to her if she were to leave this world soon. It was only a means to having a few simple pleasures before her demise occurred. Could she do that to Clay? Was she capable of leading him down that path? And was it considered using him if she actually developed true feelings for him? These were all questions Emmy asked of herself as she watched the mist come closer, surrounding the house like a gray wool blanket. Maybe her death was closer than she had thought. Realizing this brought something new to her thoughts. Along with the eerie fog, a real fear set in that she had never experienced before. She decided it would be best if she went through this alone. She would not drag Clay along with her. They could be friends, but that was all. Her heart was heavy, but if this was to be her fate, she was willing to accept it.

∞

When Clay first opened his eyes that morning, he felt full of excitement for the day to come. When he came upstairs to bed, to sleep off what was left of the night, he immediately opened the safe and held the bracelet in his hands. It sparked more than it had ever done before, and this time the sparks were a variety of colors. He took it with him to the balcony, in hopes of catching a glimpse of her again. Was it spying if she knew he looked? At this point he didn't care. He was beyond reason now. He was madly in love already. But as he approached the balcony door, he was disappointed to see that there was a heavy fog blocking his view of the yard below. Even if she was out there, he would not be able to see her at all. It also meant that what he had planned for the day would have to be put on hold, at least until this mist cleared up, and that would only happen if the sun came out to chase it away. Clay needed to see her. He simply had to.

An idea came to him as to how he could make this happen, so he walked back inside and headed toward his phone, but before he got to it, it rang. When he picked it up, he saw that the call was from London. It was from Mr. Blythe.

"Hello, Dwayne, uh, sorry, -- Mr. Blythe. How are you?"

"Good morning, Mr. Harris. I'm fine, thank you. Did I wake you? I forgot to check the time differential. I'm afraid it's a bit early for you."

"No problem. I'm out of bed, but just. I haven't had my coffee yet, so you might have to talk slowly," he joked.

There was no sound of laughter on the other end. All business, Mr. Blythe was quick to get to the point. "I've had another conversation with your mother."

"And?" asked Clay, anxiously.

"I've made some headway. She will not meet you in person, and will not tell her family about you, but I think I might be able to convince her to do a Skype conversation, privately, from our office, so you can at least see each other. She is thinking about it, but that's more than we've ever had before."

"That's great news! I would love to look at her face and hear her voice. I'm not asking to join her family circle. I'm hoping for some information about my ancestry, more than anything else."

"Yes, I understand. But I'm not sure she is convinced that's all you want."

"Please convey to her what I have expressed. I will *not* intrude on her life. I am a man of my word. She has my assurance."

"I will certainly tell her once more."

"Thank you for all you're doing, Mr. Blythe. I can rest easy knowing you are doing your best."

"That you can, sir. I'll be getting in touch with you as soon as I have any more word," said the proper Brit.

"Wonderful. Have a good day, and goodbye."

"Goodbye, sir."

After he disconnected, Clay took only a moment to consider what he had just heard. He was getting closer to finding out more about his birth parents. There was only one person he wanted to tell. He didn't think twice before he tapped in Emmy's number. He held his breath until he heard the musical tones of her voice.

"Hello?"

"Good morning, Emmy. Would you like to have breakfast with me? I hate to eat alone."

Chapter Sixteen

When Clay opened the door and saw the vision before him, the sight of her caught his breath. How was it possible that she could be even more lovely, so early in the morning, than she had been last night – soaked through, dripping hair, shivering with the cold, with the glow of the firelight as a backdrop which had been warming them both? This morning her face, clean of all makeup, was more childlike than he had seen it before. Her dark hair was long and flowing, reaching down her back to the top of her very short shorts. She wore a metal link belt with an extended end that clinked together when she moved, and her white peasant blouse was filmy and begged the viewer to peek further.

Their greeting was a bit awkward. Clay stepped forward and kissed her on the cheek. Emmy seemed surprised at his restraint. She broke the ice by saying, "What's for breakfast?"

"I thought we would start with a nice cup of English Breakfast Tea, a blueberry scone, and some poached eggs. Do you like bacon or sausage links? We'll go all American on the meat."

"Bacon, please."

"Good. One moment, please. I'll put the order in with Cook."

A giggle escaped from Emmy's lips. "Cook? Even for breakfast?"

"Why not? She's already here; I hire her full time, so I might as well use her, and besides she's a fantastic chef and baker."

The tea was served immediately, the brew set to steep the moment the cook heard he was to have a guest. "I have a question for you." said Emmy.

"Anything. What is it?"

"You don't have a job, yet you have all of this. Is there money in your family? Am I being too bold, here? None of my business?"

"No, not all. I mean about my family. Well, yes, they do have some means. My father is a successful business man. He's been slowing down as he gets older, but he's still doing quite well. As far as my money goes, it's um, well, it's inherited."

"Oh. That explains it, then. You just seemed too young to have earned all of this on your own."

"Yes, well, someday I might tell you all about it. Ah ha! Here's our breakfast." Clay was glad for the interruption.

They ate in silence for a few moments, not quite sure where this new romance/friendship was going. Then Clay began to talk about their day.

"Oh, I wasn't aware we were having 'a day.'" She laughed at his crestfallen face when she pointed out his assumption.

"I'm terribly sorry. I meant to ask you first. I really did. Would you care to spend the day with me? I have to do a bit of research for my book. I thought you might like to take a ride with me to check something out."

"Sounds interesting. Where are we going?"

"I'm writing about Father Marquette --

"Oh yes. We talked about that at the channel when we first met."

"Right, we did, and I'm still working on it. Well, anyway, I'd like to take a drive to Ludington to the place where he was first buried. There's a memorial there for him. I need to see it for myself. Would you care to go along?"

"How far is it? I have Tessie to think about."

"Does she like to ride in cars? You're more than welcome to bring her along."

"She's a great car rider. In fact, it's her favorite thing to do. Just say the word, 'ride,' and she's bouncing off the walls."

Clay grinned. "Shall we do it, then?"

Emmy decided to throw caution to the wind. It might not be fair to Clay to start a relationship, but she was badly in need of company, and her days might be few. "Let's do it. I'll just put on some long pants after breakfast and put up my hair."

"Ah, but your legs and hair are your best features. Am I to be denied the pleasure of viewing them as we drive?"

Emmy looked at him sideways, with a teasing smile. She couldn't help but flirt; he was so darned good-looking. "There'll be plenty of time for looking later, Clay."

With that look, his heart almost stopped completely. It was a bold invitation, and he was more than thrilled at the possibility.

∞

The ride to Ludington was very pleasant. After the night's rain, the world seemed clean and fresh. Light fluffy cumulus clouds made intriguing pictures against the cerulean sky. The trip took less than an hour, but it gave them enough time in the enclosed space of the car to learn more about each other. Emmy told about the relationship with her sister, and how they had been at each other as long as she could remember.

"Why do you think that is?" asked Clay, daring to plunge forward with personal questions.

Emmy sighed and thought for a moment. "I guess it all has to do with the fact that Marge's boyfriends always liked me, and she was jealous."

"Did you instigate it?"

"Of course, not. Besides, most of them were jerks, anyway. And our grandmother seemed to favor me, too, which didn't help matters."

"Why would she favor you?"

"I looked like her side of the family, and Marge looked like our dad's. Grandma never liked our dad. And although I was embarrassed sometimes even though she tried to hide her favoritism, I have to admit that I did love Grandma and her special attention. We had a very close bond."

"Has she passed away?"

Emmy was quiet for a moment. "Yes, it's been a few years ago, now."

"Sorry." Clay reached over and took her hand. He did feel compassion, but it offered him the opportunity to caress her fingers and wrap them in his.

Emmy was glad he had taken her hand. She felt comfortable with his touch. She was sure Grandma would have approved of the gentleman that Clay was. Suddenly a vision assaulted Emmy. She grabbed her head and squeezed her eyes closed.

"Emmy, what's wrong? Emmy! Talk to me." Clay quickly pulled the car over. Emmy was white as a ghost, and a sheen of perspiration had broken out on her brow.

"I'm fine," she whispered. She attempted a small laugh, but it came out as a choked sob; her heart was racing.

"Emmy, what is it?"

"Nothing at all, Clay. Let's continue to drive, okay? Please?"

"Okay. Are you sure? You don't look too good."

"Yes, I'm fine now. I just get headaches sometimes."

"Here's a bottle of water. Drink. It might help. Maybe you're just dehydrated."

"Thank you, Clay." He pulled back onto the road cautiously, watching her for signs of another attack. Emmy would never tell him that she had had a living color preview of her death and for the first time it was very clear. It most certainly did involve Clay, but looking at his concerned face, she knew it was too late to turn back. She was in over her head, and if death was to come to her soon in some way, she wanted to be with him when it happened. She gave him a weak smile of assurance, and they traveled on.

∞

The couple was happily chatting away, laughing at Tessie as she gave little whines and growls, her signal for having to go 'potty.'

"Just a minute, Tess. We're almost there. Then you can have some nice grass."

They had exited the expressway and were now traveling through country roads. They twisted and turned and twisted again. They passed farmlands and dark tunnels of trees as they headed toward Lake Michigan. And when they finally arrived, Tessie almost leapt from the car, which would have been a disaster on such short and delicate little legs. Emmy caught her in flight, hooked her up, and took her to a nice green grassy patch. Now, suddenly interested in sniffing everything in the area, all thoughts of doing what she needed to do were gone from her head.

"Hurry up, Tessie. Why must we go through this every single time? Just get it done." And finally she squatted, did her thing, and spun around looking for approval. "Good girl."

"Look, Emmy. Here's a large boulder marking the spot where he died."

"What does the plaque say?" Emmy was overcome with awe and respect, as she stood on this sacred ground.

"It says:

This Boulder Marks the Traditional Location of the Death of Pere Marquette. Revered and Loved by the Red Men. James Marquette., S. J. Noted French Missionary and Explorer. The First White Man to Reach These Shores. 1637-1676.

"It's amazing, isn't it? This is the actual spot where he died, 350 years ago."

"I'm glad someone took the time to care for this place. Look, over here, another marker. A State of Michigan Historic Site sign." This time Emmy read the large historical marker.

Marquette's Death.

Father Jacques Marquette, the great missionary and explorer, died and was buried by two French companions somewhere along the Lake Michigan shore on May 18, 1675.

He had been returning to his mission at St. Ignace, which he had left in 1673, to go exploring in the Mississippi country.

The exact location of his death has long been a subject of controversy.

A spot close to the southeast slope of the hill, near the ancient outlet of the Pere Marquette River, corresponds with the death site as located by early French accounts and maps and a constant tradition of the past.

Marquette's remains were buried at St. Ignace in 1677.

There was silence a moment as the couple took in everything they had read.

"It feels sort of reverent here, doesn't it?" whispered Emmy, almost to herself. "Even though he was young, he didn't die in vain."

"Yes, that's what fascinates me. The strength and courage that men of those times had is amazing. Diving into the unknown and not knowing what was around the next corner. His maps and journals were invaluable, and along the way he converted a lot of souls to Christianity."

"It's quite a legacy. Maybe we should learn something from him, and do more good while we're in the world."

"I think you're right, Emmy. Most of us do not do a fraction of what we could to help others. Some of us never even look at our surroundings and appreciate this beautiful world." He looked into her eyes, as they began to well with tears. Overtaken with her compassion, he had no choice but to take her in his arms and kiss her. Let the people in the nearby houses watch; he didn't care one bit.

Emmy released her lips from his, and looked into his eyes. She was sure that Clay had misread her tears. She alone knew that she did not have enough days left to do the good she had just talked about. She had wasted so much time. How had she gotten so lucky? This man was perfect for her in every way. But why now? Why was he in her life now, when she would not be in this world long enough to enjoy him. And what about him? Was it fair to let him fall in love with her? These were questions she pondered in the split second that felt like an eternity. She knew there would be no answers coming today, so the best thing for them both was to just go on with the rest of the afternoon and have some fun. She would have to sort out her moral dilemma later, probably in the long dark hours of the night.

"Come on," said Clay, tugging on her hand. "Let's climb to the top of the steps." They were standing at the base of a hill, and at the top was a large white cross – another marker for Father Marquette. The dune wasn't very high – not more than 50 steps; the two young people could easily make it, but it was a trial for little Tessie. She had to be carried part of the way. When they got to the top, they burst out in laughter.

"There's not much here, is there?" chuckled Emmy.

"No, I expected more of a view. Maybe in the fall when the leaves are off the trees, we would be able to see farther."

"Turn around. You can see Lake Michigan between the house tops. The people living here must have a great view of the water. And this way there looks like another lake down there, but there are so many tree branches I really don't see much."

"I think that's Pere Marquette Lake."

"Well, it sure could use a bit of loving care – the cross, I mean. It's due for a coat of paint, and the weeds are in need of some trimming around the base. But it's probably difficult to maintain up here. Still and all, the residents and the State have acknowledged Father Marquette as part of their heritage. That's nice."

Emmy could see by the crease in Clay's brow that he was deep in thought. She waited a moment before speaking, to give him some time. "A penny for your thoughts. What's going on in that brain of yours?"

"Oh, just thinking about my book, and how I will go about it. I haven't yet worked out my outline. I was waiting for a few more facts other than from books. You know, there's a larger and more beautiful dedication to Marquette's life and death in St. Ignace, the place of his mission and final burial -- a National Memorial, just off the expressway in town. Would you care to go with me sometime?"

"You mean across the bridge?"

"Yes, it's right in St. Ignace, not too far after you cross."

"I might be open to that. I've never crossed The Mighty Mac before."

Clay's mouth fell open. "You've never crossed the bridge?"

"No, we went to the base of it once; we stayed at the campground there when I was young. But my mom was afraid of crossing bridges. We would have to drive long distances whenever we traveled to avoid big bridges. My dad wanted to take us girls over, and leave Mom behind in the campground, but she wouldn't hear of it. She said she was afraid for us and would have nothing to do with subjecting her daughters to those awful heights over water. So it never happened. We did get to see it at night, though. It's really something when it's all lit up."

As they began the descent down, Tessie sat down and refused to budge. She made it perfectly clear what she thought of those nasty steps, so Clay carried her. "Well, we'll have to do something about your lack of bridge experience. When we get back, let's look at calendars and coordinate our schedules for another trip. It will take us four hours to get there, so we might have to stay overnight," he said softly.

They had made it to the base of the hill that housed the cross. Clay put Tessie down, so she could roam a bit before they got back into the car. "Overnight? Hmm. I don't know about that. Where would we sleep?" she teased.

"In a motel, of course," he teased back. "Better yet, let's look for a bed and breakfast. It's so much more romantic." Then he pulled her in close, wrapped his arms around her like a cocoon, and kissed her with more passion than she had felt from him before.

"Oh, my," she said, breathlessly. "Someone's been holding back. Bed and breakfast, huh? We'll see." She winked, and then she picked up Tessie to put her in the car.

Clay's heart was racing. How was it possible she could have this effect on him? One minute, she was so childlike, and the next minute she was so sexy. If it was up to him, they would head up north at this very moment and find that B&B.

Chapter Seventeen

The lazy days of summer were coming to an end. It wouldn't be long before Marge and Ken came home to claim their rights to the lake mansion once again. Emmy went to a few orientation classes for the new school system she was to work for, but so far there was no mention of a regular teaching position for her. The only way she was going to get regular work was if someone got sick or needed some time off. Her work schedule looked bleak; therefore, so did her bank account. To take her mind off of her troubles, Clay had suggested they spend as much time together as possible. There were still a lot of good weather days ahead of them, he said.

It had become their habit to share breakfast together. Most of the time they were at Clay's house, because he had a cook, but once in a while Emmy would cook for him. Today they were eating on her patio. She had already served the coffee, and was inside finishing up the rest of the meal, while Clay went over more notes for his Marquette project. To an outsider it looked as if they were a married couple, or at least two people who had been together a long time. Tessie dozed in the morning sun at Clay's side, while he flipped through papers and notebooks.

As Emmy stepped outside, she called, "Here I come. Hot and ready."

"Oh, am I having you for breakfast?"

"What?"

"You said 'hot and ready.' I thought you were giving me a heads up for what was to come."

Emmy slapped him lightly on the back with the free hand she had. "Clay. You're such a tease. I meant the pancakes, of course. Banana pancakes, real Michigan maple syrup, whip cream if you desire, and bacon – crisp, just the way you like it."

"What? No fresh-squeezed orange juice?"

"Fresh out of the carton."

"I'm disappointed in you," he teased some more. "Wow, it smells fabulous and looks fit for a king."

"Well, you're my British guy, so yes, you can be my king." She kissed him on the cheek, but as soon as she was able to put the breakfast tray down, he pulled her onto his lap, and gave her the kind of kiss he had been yearning for. They had become much closer since that trip to Ludington. Their flirtations were more intense; it wouldn't be long before their passion would need to be quenched, but so far Emmy had been holding back. It puzzled Clay, but he was willing to wait until she was ready.

"Emmy, I was thinking that today might be a good boating day. What do you think? The weather is going to be perfect. Clear skies, no wind. I haven't taken you out yet. Are you up for it?"

Emmy hesitated a moment. Everything she planned now, came with the question, 'is this the day?' After the trip to Ludington, she had decided it was best not to tell Clay about her vision. He wouldn't be able to handle it. She doubted that most people would. How could they if they knew someone they were falling in love with was going to die soon? Maybe it wasn't right not to tell him, but in her mind she was sparing him more pain than he would otherwise have to endure. She had rationalized keeping their relationship going by telling herself that she had a right to have love before it was too late for her. If her life was to be cut short, she wanted to experience some of the things other people would have during their lifetimes. Maybe it was selfish, but she had already made up her mind. She would try not to hurt Clay in the process.

"Sure, let's go. Today's a good day. If we're not gone too long, Tessie can stay home. If I ever lost her overboard, Marge would never forgive me. She calls from every port just to ask about Tess."

"When are they due back?" asked Clay, while biting into a piece of bacon. He knew that once they returned, Emmy would most likely move out; then their idyllic neighborly days would be over.

"She said the end of November, so I still have almost three months." Emmy poured syrup on her pancakes. "I must say, I won't miss being in this big house alone, but once I start teaching and get some kind of income, she'll expect me to move."

Clay reached for her hand. "Maybe we can do something about that. What do you say?"

"Clay – I – well, let's wait and see, okay?"

"Emmy, you must know how I feel about you. I love seeing you and being with you every day. Besides, you're my inspiration."

"Inspiration? For what?"

"You're always encouraging me to continue with my book. You have an interest in what I'm doing, and I love your input. I can't imagine not having you with me every day."

"Clay, I need more time. I just came out of a long relationship, remember? I want to take it slow."

"I understand. I can be patient, even if it's difficult. I plan on waiting for you, Em — however long it takes."

Emmy smiled, but she looked down to hide her tears. Clay saw her emotion and took it that she did not feel the same way he did. He could not lose her. As strange as it sounded, she had been sent to him by Gina. He knew that now. Somehow he had to find a way to prove to her they were meant to be. They were soul mates.

∞

As Clay had predicted, it was a perfect boating day. They drove the Sapphire C slowly around Muskegon Lake, enjoying the view of the houses from the lake side, and since the waves were so calm, they ventured out through the channel and went into Lake Michigan. As soon as they cleared the breakwater, the waves were a little larger, but it was nothing Clay's new boat couldn't handle with ease. Emmy loved the rocking motion. That along with the warm sun, lulled her into a lazy stupor. Clay thoroughly enjoyed watching her lovely body stretched out for an end-of-summer tan, while he was at the helm maneuvering the waves. Once he was well away from shore and clear of other boats in the area, he turned off the motor and dropped the anchor. He stripped off his shirt and joined Emmy, lying next to her in the sun's golden rays. Emmy peeked through her lashes when she heard his movements. Pleasantly surprised to see how fit and trim he was, she sat up and smiled invitingly. Clay came to her eagerly, and with no watching eyes anywhere near, they were free to explore each other, as all lovers do.

Clay loved having her in his arms, her hot skin next to his. He reached up and released the clip she had in her hair and let the long dark strands fall around his face as he pulled her down onto him. "Emmy, Emmy my love," said Clay, in between kisses, first of her luscious mouth and then her neck. Although it was difficult to do, he had to accomplish something before they went any further. In between nibbles, he whispered, "I have something I want to give you."

"You do, do you?" she said suggestively.

"Well, yes, I was hoping. But just a minute, it's a gift." He hated tearing himself away from her, but this next step would be crucial in their relationship. If he was wrong, it would change everything, so he presented her with the lovely dark blue velvet box he had purchased just for this occasion.

"Oh, my, the box alone is a beautiful present. Maybe I don't need to bother looking inside," she teased.

"Open it. I have waited from the day I first met you to give this to you." Clay's heart was pounding. His life hinged on how she reacted.

When Emmy opened the box, the breath she sucked in was audible, because she was looking at the most beautiful thing she had ever seen. The diamonds sparkled in the sun, and the sapphires glowed with the reflection of the azure sky and cobalt water.

"Oh, Clay. It's too much. I can't accept it."

"Yes, you can. I want you to have it."

She reached out to touch the jewels, and harmless sparks flew off of it like fireworks. She jumped and almost dropped it, but Clay was quick and caught it midair.

"What just happened?" she asked.

"Exactly what I hoped. It *was* meant for you, I knew it." He placed the bracelet on her wrist and fastened it, and the sparks went wild. Once it was secure, he kissed her more fervently than ever before. What was even better is that she responded, and when their eyes locked, they could not tear them away from each other. The moment the clasp was fastened, their desire heightened, and Clay was lost, as if he was falling into the depths of her soul. As they rose to go to the cabin below, in unspoken mutual consent, the bracelet sent out sparks of blue and yellow and orange and red.

Emmy wasn't sure what was happening, but all she knew was that she needed Clay. She had to have Clay. She wanted Clay and would always want Clay. He would be the only one for her, for however long she had left, now and forever.

Chapter Eighteen

The couple lay entwined in each other's arms, still breathing heavily. They were both in awe at what had just happened to them. They kissed again and again, and it wasn't long before Clay wanted more.

"Whoa," said Emmy, with a laugh. "What just happened?"

"What do you mean, my sweet?" asked Clay, while giving her little love bites.

"Clay, please sit up."

"Oh, of course." Clay was suddenly aware that she was no longer teasing. The tone of her voice had changed. She was seriously pushing him away.

Emmy paused a moment before she dared to say what she was thinking. "I can truthfully say I have never experienced anything like what just happened between us in my life. Don't get me wrong, it was awesome, incredible, and yes, I want more, but did you give me a drug or something? What was that?" When she looked into his eyes, she felt like she was drowning in his soul, and she knew one thing for sure -- she still had an intense desire to kiss him again and start all over. He was so sweet and so handsome and so sexy. Her breathing began to quicken as her pulse raced erratically.

Clay saw the look in her eyes, and started to caress her silky skin, but she somehow had the strength of mind to gently push him away. "Hold on, sailor. Let's talk," she said softly, with one last kiss.

With a sigh, Clay reached over and took the bracelet off of her wrist. He saw Emmy's hurt look, and before he could explain, she said, "Was the bracelet just a bribe for sex? Is that it? If I don't put out again, you're taking it back? Clay, how could you think that of me?"

"Wait. Wait a minute. That's not it, at all. I need to explain, but when I do, you have to listen to me until I'm done speaking. No interruptions, okay?"

Emmy studied him with tears in her eyes. She seemed to be constantly tearing up in his presence. She'd never been a weak woman before, but Clay had turned her to mush. She had thought he was the most honest and sincere man she had ever met, but now she was so confused she didn't know what to think. Maybe men with money were all like this.

"Can I tell you a story?" he asked.

"A story? You're kidding me, right?"

"No, I'm dead serious."

When she heard him utter the word 'dead,' she shuddered. He reached for an afghan and threw it over her shoulders thinking she was cold, although covering her nakedness was the last thing he wanted to do. Clay took her hands in his and began to caress her fingers as he told her the story of his trip to England to find his mother. He related all of the details about the gypsy he had met in a shop on a rainy London day. He watched as her eyes grew larger, and when he said the phrase the gypsy had murmured to him, she gasped.

"Her very words were, *she will call you by your childhood name. She belongs to me, and therefore I belong to you,*" Clay repeated. And when he told Emmy about how he had watched her from his balcony while holding the bracelet and how the bracelet had produced sparks, he saw her eyes change from disbelieving to surprise to shock. He could see how she was taking it all in, so as her brain tried to decipher it all, he stopped talking long enough for her to come to grips with his tale.

"Now, what do you think? Am I crazy?" If she rejected him, Clay would not be able to handle it. He waited patiently until she was able to speak.

"Oh, Clay, oh Clay, my darling," she cried, as she threw her arms around his neck and sobbed.

He didn't care what had brought on this response. Just the fact that she was not turning him away was enough for now.

When Emmy was finally able to pull herself away, she smiled sweetly, and said, "Now, it's my turn to tell you a tale of gypsies."

It took her a little longer to tell her story, and when she was through, with quiet ceremony, Clay placed the bracelet back on her wrist. "It may not be a crown, but it is yours now and forever, my queen." Then they fell back into the covers and made passionate love once more, as the boat rocked and the sparks flew.

∞

"What do we do now, my love?" asked Emmy lazily, as Clay traced a pattern on her skin, making goosebumps rise, while sending pleasant sensations to all the right places.

"I have a suggestion, but first I need to ask if you have ever read any books by Ivy Morton?"

"Books? Well, I do read a lot and I have started to read Ruby and Sal, but I'm not very far into it."

"You need to read her whole series, one after another, and then we'll talk about this again." He kissed her nose, caressed her cheek, and went up top to start up the motor and raise anchor, so they could return to shore.

∞

Clay stood on his balcony breathing in deeply of the fresh morning air. His silk robe hung open, exposing his bare, unshaven, chest to the day. It had rained early in the morning while he slept, creating a gentle pitter-patter rhythm that had soothed his soul. The earth felt fresh and new again; the smell was so sweet that he inhaled until his lungs could hold no more. He couldn't get enough of it, just like he would never get enough of Emmy. He smiled, remembering their time on the boat and the love they had shared.

After docking the boat, two days ago, Emmy had parted with Clay by asking that he not contact her until she had read the books and had had time to digest them and to think about what they had learned about each other. He had held true to his word that he would wait for her to call him, but it had been torture. He stretched over the railing in order to see all of the patio next door, and he was now assured that she was not outside. Walking back in, he started to go to the safe to look once more at the sapphires, as had been his habit for the past few months, but with a chuckle, he remembered that the one they truly belonged to was in possession of the gems now. Clay was positive that as long as she owned the bracelet, she would always be his, so he was not worried that she would not call; it was just a matter of time. When the phone finally did ring, he grabbed it quickly, but it was not the one he had been waiting for. He touched the green dot and listened for the now familiar accent.

"Hello, Mr. Harris. How have you been?"

"Hello, Mr. Blythe. All is well here, and you?"

"The same. Yes, the same, thank you."

"Are you calling with news for me?" asked Clay getting right to the point.

He heard Mr. Blythe's intake of breath, and assuming it meant the worst, he was totally unprepared for what was said next. "I believe we have convinced her to have a video chat. Now, don't get too excited, she may still back down. But it seems as though she has begun to get curious about you."

"Really! I'm shocked. I never thought you would get this far with her. Of course, I still am not sure what I want to accomplish except to know that she is well, and that she thinks of me on occasion."

"Yes, well she is and does. Now when would you like to arrange this little conference, and do you want anyone present? I'll be glad to be a monitor; or perhaps you'll need privacy." Clay almost laughed at how Mr. Blythe pronounced privacy with a short 'i'. He wasn't making fun of it, because he himself said it that way often; he had had to work long and hard to drop his British way of pronouncing certain words, but it did seem to surface once in a while. He noticed that after he had a conversation with Mr. Blythe, it came back stronger than ever.

"Perhaps you can be there to start, and then leave us alone for a few moments, if she agrees."

"I'm sure she will. She seems almost eager, now. Is there a specific day that works better than others?" asked Mr. Blythe, in his most official voice.

"No, not at all. Let her determine when. I will make myself available to her schedule."

"Wonderful. I'll get back to you soon. And Michael, stay near the phone. It could be later today."

Clay smiled at hearing himself called Michael once again. It had been a while and he was already so used to Clay that Michael now sounded foreign to his ears. But he really didn't care what Mr. Blythe called him; as long as this video chat went through, he was happy to answer to anything.

Clay was truly tense now. He was not only waiting to see how Emmy would handle what she read in Ivy's books about the ruby necklace, but now he was waiting on pins and needles to hear from Fiona, his birth mother. As he was descending the stairs to get a second cup of coffee, the phone rang again. He couldn't get it out of his pocket fast enough. His fingers seemed to be too fat the reach into his pocket and grab ahold of the thing. He finally got it out, just in time to see that it was from neither of the two he was waiting to hear from. The call was from Ivy.

"Good morning, Clay. How are you?"

"Ivy, so good to hear from you. I'm fine, and more importantly how are you?"

"I'm good, and so are the children and Fox. All is well here."

"And the pregnancy is going well, I presume?"

"Yes, it is," laughed Ivy. "I almost wished I hadn't told so many people right away. It seems like an eternity before she arrives. We were just so excited to increase our family, so we blurted the news. But, listen, I was not calling to talk about my new arrival in the spring. I've been thinking about what you had asked me at your house that day -- about you-know-what. Are there any new developments? Just curious."

Clay was now in the kitchen, getting himself another cup of coffee. He walked out to the patio, careful not to spill his hot mug, and hoping to keep this conversation away from the hired help. "It's so strange that you should ask. Yes, there have been some new developments. I would like to get together with you soon, and I may be bringing someone with me."

"Now, Clay, that conversation was just between you and me, and of course I told Fox. I can't share it with anyone else, and I will deny anything we discussed."

"I haven't told her anything, yet, except about how I came to own the bracelet. I just asked her to read your books. And when she does she will have questions, I'm sure. I can only say to you, that I have shown her my sapphire bracelet, and it works – if you know what I mean. I gave it to her. She's the one." Clay chuckled, embarrassed at what he was saying to Ivy.

"Oh," said Ivy thoughtfully. And then "Oh, my!" she exclaimed. "Well, then, that might be a different story. Let me discuss this with Fox, and I'll get back to you. This could mean any number of things. Clay. We have to be careful."

"Yes, I completely understand. Please get back to me soon. There are a lot of things that need to be cleared up."

"Yes, I guess there are. Well, have a good day, Clay. This was a very interesting talk."

"Bye, Ivy, I'll be waiting to hear from you." He touched the red dot and disconnected, then he held his phone a moment, staring at the screen, wondering what was to come next.

Chapter Nineteen

"Michael, she will be at my office in one hour for a video chat. If you get this message, call immediately."

Clay could not believe he had missed the call. There was just so much going on. He had stepped outside for some fresh air, hoping to hear Emmy's voice through the hedge, and he had left his phone inside. As soon as he came in, he realized his mistake and checked for missed calls. That's when he found the message. Over thirty minutes had already passed. How could he be so stupid? He dialed Mr. Blythe's office number, and it was answered by his secretary. As soon as he said his name, he was connected to the inner office.

"Michael, I'm so glad you called. She's here already and believe me, she's very nervous and ready to leave. Let me calm her down and then we'll place the Skype call. Give me your Skype number, then, for Heaven's sake, make sure your computer is on."

"Yes, of course. And thank you, Mr. Blythe." Michael ran to his desk in his office, and set the computer for the best angle and light, then he made sure he had a tablet and pen in case he had to write something down. "Maria," he called, "please make sure I am not interrupted." Then he closed the door.

The next few moments were agonizing, but finally there were the familiar tones of a Skype call coming through. Clay watched as Mr. Blythe gave the shy woman instructions on how best to use Skype. He told her to speak clearly and face the small camera in the computer, then he stepped out of the picture and left mother and son alone for the first time since Clay's birth. She seemed afraid to speak, so Clay took the reins, and said, "Hello, my name is Michael Clayton Harris the Third, but you can call me Clay."

"Hello," she said, softly. "I'm Fiona Andover McMurtry, your mother. It's nice to meet you."

"And you, too. I want to thank you for agreeing to see me like this. I know it's hard for you, but it really means a lot to me."

Fiona smiled weakly, holding back tears. "This is very difficult for me. I want to thank you for understanding that. I hope you know it has nothing to do with you. It's just that I have a family now, three sons and a husband, and they don't know about you."

Clay grinned. "I have three more brothers? That's amazing."

"Yes, but I don't want you to try to contact them. They're still young yet – teenagers – and they wouldn't understand. They might look at me differently."

"Yes, I understand. I would never do anything to make you ill at ease or to upset your family. I am more interested in who you are, my background, genetically and genealogically. And maybe some ancestors' names. Can you tell me anything about yourself?"

"There's not much to tell, Clay. I come from simple people. We work hard for a living, but I was always told to be truthful. I was taught to be a good Christian, so that is why I agreed to meet you. I know you have questions. I will try my best, but some I may not be able to answer."

"Thank you, I appreciate it more than you can ever know. I was told your last name is McMurtry, now. It's your husband's name, I presume."

"Yes, it is. He's Irish -- an immigrant when he was a child."

Clay hesitated a moment before he asked the next question. "Do you know anything about my biological father?" It pained Clay to see the color drain from her face.

"That's territory I didn't want to have to visit ever again, but I see that it is something you don't want to give up on. I'll say it once and then I'll never speak of it again. As you know from the letter I left you -- you did get it, right?"

"Yes, I did, so I know how hurtful this is for you, but you see, I have a good reason for asking, or I would never intrude on your privacy."

"Yes, yes, I can see that now. You are a kind and considerate man. But unfortunately your father was not. He was an old family friend, or so we all thought. He was not a stranger as I wrote to you. I was only 15, and he was 40. I was afraid something would leak about his existence, so I lied. One night, when I was home alone, he came to visit when my parents weren't home. Looking back, I'm sure he knew all along they would not be there. I thought it was okay to let him in and serve him some tea, but it wasn't long before he tricked me into showing him my room. He raped me there, and even though I fought, he was strong; he used so much force I could not resist. I had to hide what happened from my parents, because he was my da's best friend. When they soon discovered my pregnancy, they assumed I had been with a boy my age, and life was very difficult from then on. Times were hard for us, financially, I had younger brothers and sisters, and so my parents made me give the child, you, away. There were just too many mouths to feed. I went away with a friend, so the younger children would not know about my pregnancy. I was young at the time, and I hate to say it, but I thought I would be relieved, and that I could forget the shame if I never saw my baby's face again, but it never did work out that way." Fiona paused to blow her nose and wipe tears. "I never forgot about you, and when I had my first born with my husband, and felt a mother's love, I truly regretted what I had done for the first time. But now it's too late. No one, other than my parents and my best friend and her mother, knew about you. I never told a soul the rapist's name."

"I'm so sorry to hear all of this, and it shames me, also, to know that my father was this kind of a man. I am sorry to even ask this, but will you tell me his name? You know I will never bring it up with your family, ever. But I need to know my ancestry. It is important, now more than when I first started on this quest. I can't explain to you the reason why, but, Fiona, I pride myself on being a man of integrity. I have no intention of ever trying to contact him. You can trust me."

Fiona broke down and cried hard, then. She studied his face in the monitor, and shortly her face changed and Clay could see she had come to some conclusion.

"I will tell you his name, but then I will never mention it again. I can never have contact with you after today, and you have to promise to never seek out my children, even after I'm gone. If you agree, I will utter his name one time, and one time only."

Clay was disappointed that he could not have any more contact with her, but right now, finding out about his ancestry was of the utmost importance. With a heavy heart he agreed to her terms.

"His name is Artem Karpenko. I don't know anything about his family. Now, I must go; my family does not know I am here." And with that she clicked off, not even saying goodbye.

Clay was left looking at a blank screen, and with an ache in his heart. His mother seemed to be a sweet woman, but she had a life that did not include him, and now with the agreement they had made, it never would. He felt empty, but that feeling was nothing new. He had been experiencing it ever since he moved to Muskegon and started the classes. But there was one thing that was new. He had his birth father's name. He was not a man to be proud of, that's for sure, but nonetheless the name 'Karpenko' might lead him to some answers. He was sure he had heard it before, and if he was right, it was a name Ivy had used in one of her books. Another meeting with her was in order, but would she tell him what he needed to know?

Chapter Twenty

Emmy closed the last of Ivy Morton's books. She didn't know what to think about what she had just read. A few days ago, she would have been sure that it was a fiction book and therefore every word she read was a figment of the author's imagination. But after that wonderfully, fantastic afternoon on the Sapphire C with Clay, and after he had presented her with the beautiful sapphire and diamond bracelet, she wasn't sure of anything, anymore. Was she so overwhelmed with the gift that she had lost all her senses? Because what they had experienced after he placed it on her wrist was nothing like she had ever experienced before. Could she truly be so easily bought with sparkles and flash? Was she that shallow? If there was one thing Emmy was sure of, was that she knew herself very well. Yes, she was a girl, and yes, she liked pretty new things, but she had always thought that baubles could never buy her. She had proven that to boys through her teen years over and over again. And when she grew into womanhood, she had rejected gifts on many occasions, because she knew they came with strings attached.

Emmy shook her head to clear her thoughts. Her dark sleek hair fell forward like a curtain, draping perfectly into place around her shoulders. She touched her wrist where the bracelet had been. Clay had insisted that she keep it, but she was afraid to wear it. If the magic were real, what would happen if she wore the thing in public? Would she attack any male that came along, or was it just meant for Clay, the way the ruby necklace worked for Anya and Bo, Edward and Clara, Maisy and Max, and Ruby and Sal? And if all of that were true, who owned that ruby necklace now? Did Ivy actually have such a thing in her possession? The questions were swirling. Emmy needed answers, but she was also afraid of what she might learn, because when she was telling Clay her story, she had held nothing back about her grandmother's legacy of visions, except for one thing. She had not told him of the latest and most frequent one – her very own death.

In the beginning, Emmy had only intended on having a summer fling with Clay. She had hoped she could pretend she was in love and have that experience before she died, but she never expected to fall head over heels in love with Clay. And now if – no, *when* she died, he would be so hurt. She knew how he felt about her. She could tell it was real for him. No man had ever made love to her like that before. When she left this Earth, it would crush him. The only option was to end it, before his attachment went any further.

Taking a deep breath, Emmy let the air out of her lungs with a loud sigh which morphed into a sob. Wiping streaming tears from her cheeks, she made a decision. She would call him and tell him it was over.

She would lead him to believe he was not the man for her. And when Marge and Ken returned she would move, maybe to another state, somewhere where he could no longer find her. Then she would spend the rest of her days alone, so no one else would get hurt. Her grandmother had warned her that with knowledge of the future came pain, and she had prepared her for such a time as this. But no one could truly be prepared for the agony and loss she was about to feel.

She swung her legs over the edge of the bed and retrieved a paper she kept in the bottom of her jewelry box. It was an old list her grandmother had given her, a list of names that had meant nothing to her before except to tie her to what she had thought was a fairytale told by a fanciful woman who enjoyed entertaining her granddaughter. After hearing Clay's story of the gypsy in London, and reading a similar story in Ivy's books, she began to believe that her grandmother had been telling the truth. Maybe there was a curse on them, and the only way to eliminate the curse was to right a wrong, but she would not be the one to complete the task for the family.

She did not have the strength of character it took to accomplish such a task. She was weak, she knew that now, and that was something she would never have thought of herself before Clay came into her life. He needed to be protected, and that was the only task she was interested in.

Emmy picked up the yellowed piece of paper that had been given to her in secret; a lone tear dropped on the page leaving a watermark next to her name. This list was meant to be kept from her parents' eyes, and she had done just as her grandmother had asked. They never knew the stories the two had shared of Emmy's gypsy heritage. As Emmy traced her finger down the list and began to read the names, one by one, starting with herself, she recalled her grandmother's veined and wrinkled hands doing the same.

Emmaline Regina Simmons – Gypsy Princess

Naomi Regina (Queenie) Holmes Simmons -- Emmy's mother

Kezia Regina White Holmes – Emmy's grandmother

Regina Sorenson White – great-grandmother

Yana Regina Andrushkev Sorenson (1895) – 2x great-grandmother, and her sister Yulia Regina Andrushkev Karpenko (1900)

Regina also known as Gina (1879) Ukraine – 3x great-grandmother

Gina (1860) Ukraine – 4x great-grandmother

Gina (1845) Ukraine – 5x great-grandmother

Gina (1820) Ukraine – 6x great-grandmother, lover to Stas Karpenko, King of the Gypsies, but never married.

It was the female line that her grandmother had stressed was so important to remember. Emmy had always known that she carried the name of Regina in her blood, and she had always been told she was a princess, but until a few days ago, she had thought it was a story meant for a little girl's imagination. But as she read about a Gina in Ivy's books, she had started to tremble. Even the mention of Stas Karpenko was there in the last book. He was Bo's father, and Bo was Anya's love; they were two star-crossed lovers that people had been singing about in a folksong for generations. It was real. It must be real. It was too much of a coincidence. Stas and the first Gina had also been lovers it seemed, but fate had taken their chance away from them in some way no one would ever know now, too much time had passed. Stas had married Olnya, Bo's mother, instead. Perhaps the ruby necklace had more power than the sapphire bracelet, and future generations were forever altered, but it had not changed the fact that Emmy carried the blood of all her ancestral Ginas in her veins. She had been told by her loving grandmother that it was her job to right the wrongs of the past, a heavy burden for a young girl. But she was grown now, and it was time.

Perhaps the bracelet was meant to initiate her consummation with Clay, for some reason, and she had accomplished that. If so, it was the best job she had ever had. She didn't know what else she was meant to do, so now she would continue on with her life, alone, and leave him to wonder what went wrong. It was better than what

he would have to deal with if she stayed. This way only
one heart would be broken.

Chapter Twenty-one

The wait was killing him. He had not heard from her in a week. How long did it take for someone to read a few books, he wondered? He couldn't stand it any longer, so he decided instead of a call, maybe just a simple text would be appropriate.

"Where is that stupid phone?" said Clay out loud, looking under couches and cushions.

"Mr. Harris, do you need something?" asked Maria.

"I can't seem to find my phone. Have you seen it?"

"No, I haven't, Mr. Harris. Let me call you." The cook had been preparing a few meals for the freezer, so Clay would have something on the days she wasn't there. She took her own phone out of her pocket and called him. They could hear a faint ringing tone, but it was difficult to determine where it was coming from. They both walked around the lower level of the house listening for the little ditty that normally irritated him. Clay moved closer to the slider door off the patio. He thought he heard something, and as soon as he opened the door, the ringing tone was loud and clear.

"I found it, Maria. I left it out here when I had my coffee."

"Good to know, Mr. Harris."

Relieved to have found the phone, he now had a decision to make. Would he call her, or wait as he had promised? Feeling that a text wasn't as intrusive as a call, he went ahead with it.

"Morning. Have you finished the books yet? No pressure."

Emmy's phone made a single ding. She looked at the screen and frowned. He had put her in a position of either acknowledging him or ignoring him, and she wasn't quite ready for that, yet. She hesitated, but finally typed, "I'm done."

"Care to discuss it?"

Emmy knew that as soon as she saw Clay she would weaken. She loved him more than her own life. It was the reason she had to stay away from him. She could not be responsible for his pain.

She answered, "Not ready yet."

"Can I answer any questions?"

"No, thank you. I'm good."

Clay was a wreck. What had gone wrong? All he had asked was for her to read the books, so they could discuss some ideas and decide what it all meant. Why was she pulling away? He didn't understand. He couldn't let this happen.

"I'm coming over," he typed.

"Don't."

"Why not?"

"I can't explain."

'That's it,' he thought, and he called her number. It rang and rang until it finally went to voice mail.

At the same time that Emmy's phone was ringing, her heart was breaking. She couldn't stand the sound, so she turned off her phone. She would never listen to the message he left. She walked into her room and packed a bag. Ken and Marge were scheduled to come home later today; they had called to say they were on their way. Marge was missing Tessie and wanted to come home early, so Emmy would be free to leave. Her dog sitting and house sitting duties were over. Not caring to give a big explanation to Marge about where she was going and why, she left a note on the table and told her exactly what time she had left the house, and when Tessie had last eaten and been taken for a walk. She took only the bare essentials, because she would not need much, anyway. She reached for the bracelet, caressed it, put it on, looked lovingly at her arm, and took it off again; then she tossed it back in the drawer. A few weak sparks bounced off of it, and then it lost its luminous glow. It was now just a simple bracelet of dull blue stones surrounded by foggy white crystals.

Emmy had no idea where she was going. It didn't matter anyway. The end was near. She would not have long to wait. She had not had enough time to produce an heir, so she was the end of the long line of Gypsy princesses named Gina, and no one would miss her, except maybe Clay. He would hurt for a few days and then go on with his life. He would find other girls to share the Sapphire C with. He would produce heirs with someone else. With that image in her mind, she clutched her chest, bent over, and sobbed.

∞

In a short amount of time Emmy was packed up and driving on US31 heading north. She had one last thing she wanted to accomplish before it was too late. She was going to cross the Mackinac Bridge, the Mighty Mac; the longest suspension bridge in the Western Hemisphere.

It would not be as much fun as it would have been with Clay, but at least she could mark it off of her bucket list before she actually kicked the bucket. She chuckled a little bit at her own joke.

∞

At the exact same time that she was thinking about the bridge, Clay was pounding on her door. He realized how foolish he had been to use texting. They needed to talk face-to-face. Thinking she must be afraid of what she had read, and how it might relate to them, he had walked next door. Going around the hedges, he knocked on the patio door, and when no one answered, he peeked inside. Tessie was on the other side, wagging her tail. Never much of a watch dog, she was just happy to have company. Deciding Emmy must be upstairs, he walked around to the front door where he could use the doorbell, but as he rounded the corner of the house, he saw an empty spot where she always parked her car.

Now in a panic, he ran to the door and rang the bell over and over, knowing it was already too late. She was gone, maybe just for errands, he assured himself. He slowly walked back to his house. He would wait all day if he had to.

"Emmy," he whispered.

∞

Emmy was driving at a steady pace; she never liked to speed. Not more than a few miles past the Shelby exit, it had started to drizzle, so her windshield wipers were gently moving back and forth across her view. She was in the right lane, trying to block out what she was doing. Leaving Clay was just too painful to think about. When she came up to a slow moving truck, she stayed behind it awhile, but soon she became impatient. She put on her blinker and started to pass, but in the gray light of the day, the huge semi never saw her small silver car. The slowest moving vehicle was actually in front of the semi, and the truck driver was getting impatient, too. He changed lanes at the exact same time as Emmy, and as his huge tires brushed her car, he pushed her over. Her car slid off the road, hit the grass, and then flipped four times, ending upside down in the meridian. Everything inside the car bounced around like ping pong balls. Glass broke into tiny shards, sheet metal crinkled like cardboard, and wheels buckled underneath the frame. One tire flew off into the air as if someone had thrown a Frisbee. Emmy's head hit the side window first, then bounced forward toward the steering wheel. Even the airbags could not prevent her injuries. She was unaware of people calling her. She never heard the sirens, and the emergency vehicles arriving on the scene. A Jaws of Life tool was used to open up the car, peeling back the metal like it was a tin can. One of the EMTs cradled her with his arms as they cut the seatbelt straps to remove her limp and lifeless body. She was still breathing, but her pulse was extremely weak, and then her heart gave out. They put the paddles on her right at the scene and were able to get a weak pulse back, but she was barely hanging on. A tourniquet was tightened on her arm to stem the flow of blood coming from a large gash, and a bandage was wrapped around her head to cover a deep wound. It immediately filled with blood. Within a few minutes, she was placed on the gurney and airlifted to Mercy Hospital in Muskegon. While still in the air, an alarm went off alerting the EMTs that she was coding again. It took two more shocks until they were able to bring her back to life. Upon arrival a group of doctors and nurses rushed to work on her, hooking her up to life-saving equipment, then taking her to surgery to stitch and repair torn flesh and broken bones. After searching through her phone, a nurse found a number listed under ICE -- In Case of Emergency.

Marge was called and was given the bad news. The Thompsons' plane had just arrived at the Grand Rapids airport. It took them over an hour to get their luggage, pay for their long term parking and collect their car, then it was another 45 minutes to the hospital. After checking in at the hospital, and hearing the seriousness of the Emmy's injuries, they knew now that it was all in God's hands. There was nothing for them to do but pray. Ken left Marge for a few minutes, and raced home to take care of Tessie. They had no idea how long she had been left alone. He would come back as soon as he had unpacked the car and taken care of the little dog. Luckily, the hospital was only 20 minutes away. It was going to be a long night.

∞

At the exact moment of the crash, Clay felt a sharp pain in his stomach and heard a loud noise in his head. It sounded like metal and glass. He doubled over, got dizzy as if he was in a tumbled spin, then he turned white and almost passed out. When Maria saw him, she led him to the couch and made him sit down. She brought him some hot tea and aspirin. He took a few sips of the whiskey-laced brew and collapsed on the couch in a deep sleep. Thinking he was sick with the flu, she covered him with an afghan and left the house.

Chapter Twenty-two

Clay watched the house next door for three days. He knocked several times but there was never an answer. He called and texted frequently, but got no response. He couldn't figure out why Emmy had cut him out of her life so suddenly. He began to get worried about Tessie, as it seemed no one was taking care of her; yet each time he peeked in a window, she looked healthy and seemed happy. Finally, one day Clay was on his balcony watching the backyard once again for any sign of Emmy, when he saw a man with Tessie on a leash. Had Emmy taken on a new lover? He couldn't bear the thought of it. He slipped into his shoes and ran down the steps, out the patio door, around the hedges, and caught him just as he was going inside.

"Excuse me," he called. "Excuse me, can I talk to you for a moment?"

"What? Oh," said Ken, when he heard the voice from the hedges.

"Sorry, I didn't mean to startle you. I'm your neighbor, Clay Harris."

"Oh, yes, of course." Ken seemed quite distracted and perhaps a little annoyed at the interruption. The two men shook hands, but in his hurry to get back to the hospital, Ken had forgotten to introduce himself.

"And you are?" asked Clay.

"Oh, I'm uh, I'm Ken Thompson."

Relieved to hear the name of the man who actually owned the house and Emmy's brother-in-law, Clay smiled. "Oh yes, of course. Nice to meet you. I thought you weren't coming home for another month."

"Marge got a little homesick, so we cut it short."

"I see. Well, I've gotten to know your sister-in-law, Emmy, while you were gone. Quite well in fact. We've spent a lot of time together this summer. Can you tell me if she's home? I haven't seen her in a while."

Ken frowned and looked like he was fighting back tears. "I guess you haven't heard," he said softly.

Clay was really concerned now, as he watched Ken struggle to keep his composure. "What? What happened?" he asked.

"Emmy was in a serious accident."

"Is she okay? Where is she?" Clay felt panic set in. Emmy was in trouble, and he had not known about it. How was that possible? No one thought to tell him, but then why would they?

"No, she's not okay. She's stable for now, but it's only because she is in a medically induced coma."

"A coma? Where? I need to see her."

"She's at Mercy Hospital. But she's in ICU. She can't have visitors."

Clay had not heard a word after the word 'Mercy.' He was already running for his car. The drive seemed to take an eternity, and then he had to find a parking space. With the new construction which was adding many new floors and other renovations of the hospital going on, the parking situation was horrible. Once he found a spot, he slammed his door and ran to the main entrance. The man at the front desk, informed him that Emmy Simmons was in ICU on the third floor, and she was stable at this time, but she was not able to see anyone but immediate family members.

"Can I go up and talk to family members? I need to know how she is."

"Yes, of course," he said. "Take the elevator up to 3, then follow the red line to the ICU desk. Someone there will direct you to the family lounge."

"Thank you," and he took off running again.

When he got to the family lounge, he found a lone woman, all by herself. She was wiping her eyes with a Kleenex, while talking on her cell phone. She looked up, as she became aware of a man approaching her. She said into the phone, "He's here now. Okay, I'll talk to you in a few minutes, hon."

"Sorry," choked out Clay. Seeing Marge's tears terrified him. "I'm so sorry to intrude, but are you Marge?"

"Yes, I am. You must be Emmy's friend."

"Yes, I'm Clay Harris, your neighbor. Emmy and I met while you were gone. How is she? What happened?"

"Please sit, Clay. Emmy was in a serious accident. A semi ran her off the road, and her car flipped several times. She sustained a serious head injury, as well as a bad gash on her arm, and multiple smaller cuts. She also has a broken tibia and femur."

Clay turned white at hearing Emmy's condition. "But how is she doing? Is she okay?"

Marge began to cry, not able to hold it back any longer. "Her body will be fine once everything is healed, but it's the TBI, they call it, that's the problem."

"TBI? What is that?" asked Clay, not sure he wanted to hear the answer.

"It means traumatic brain injury."

"Brain injury? Is she going to be okay?"

"We don't know, Clay. There was swelling on her brain, so they put her in the coma. They had to remove part of her skull to relieve the pressure. At some point they will try to take her out of the coma. At that time, she could stay in a coma on her own, or she could come out of it. The doctors said it takes time. For some people it can be days and for others it's months before they come around. And of course," she hesitated to say the words, "some never do come out of it."

"Can I see her?" asked Clay, with tears in his eyes.

"I don't think they'll allow it," she said kindly. "But I'll ask. I take it that you were close with Emmy, then?"

"Yes, I am. I'm hopelessly in love with her."

Marge raised her eyebrows. "But does or did she know that? Because Daniel comes every day. He never mentioned that she was seeing someone else."

"She broke up with him shortly after you left town. We've been together ever since."

"I see," said Marge. "Oh, here's Ken."

Marge's husband gave her a kiss, then sat down next to Clay. "Any change?"

"The same – she's the same."

"But she's alive. Hold onto that Marge," he said across Clay.

Clay suddenly felt out of place. He went back to the desk and looked for someone who could give him permission to see Emmy. A nurse went to the lounge, and asked Marge and Ken if they knew Clay, after which he was granted a few moments alone with the patient.

When Clay went into the room, and saw Emmy lying on the bed with tubes and machines connected to her, he almost passed out. She had a white turban around her head, her eye was swollen shut and black and blue, her arm was bandaged, and her leg was in a cast. The blood pressure and heart monitor machines beeped as the ventilator worked her lungs, pushing air in and out in a steady rhythm. She was so still, it was difficult to believe she was alive.

Clay kissed her cheek and whispered her name, "Emmy, Emmy my love, come back to me. I can't live without you. Please Emmy, come back." He stared at her for a few seconds, but when he saw no sign of movement, he buried his face in her neck and cried.

Chapter Twenty-three

One day rolled into another. Clay was afraid to leave the hospital at first, but after a while it was necessary. Marge and Ken took shifts, and coordinated their visits with Clay. They had been extremely understanding, considering they had not even known about him until they had first met in the hospital waiting room. Daniel Luca, Emmy's previous boyfriend, had stopped by on more than one occasion when Clay was there. He was a little jealous at first, after seeing that Clay was always there. He had often wondered if Emmy had found someone before she had broken it off with him. Looking at the devastation in Clay's eyes, he could see how much he loved Emmy, and even though Daniel would never get over losing Emmy, he had conceded that Emmy probably loved Clay in a way she had never loved him. Besides, Daniel had let no grass grow under his feet. He was in a relationship himself now, although not a serious one at this time, because Daniel had never been serious about anything in his life.

After breaking up, Daniel and Emmy had continued to have phone conversations regularly. They had been friends for their entire lives, and had decided they would never break that bond. Emmy felt more like a sister now, and he did not want to lose her any more than Clay did. They had always told each other everything, but Emmy had never mentioned Clay, which probably meant he was important to her and she wanted to keep their relationship private. After working his way through all of these scenarios, Daniel had switched gears and decided if Emmy loved Clay, he would learn to like him. The two men had one shared interest, if nothing else; they both wanted Emmy to come back to them.

∞

Clay was in the shower, reflecting back on the past two weeks. If he had not had a housekeeper and a cook, he would be a total wreck. The two women who were in his house on regular occasions made sure he ate and had clean clothes. Recently, Maria had convinced him to not go to the hospital for such extended periods of time. He needed his rest, and he had to keep going on with his life, she said. He needed to stay strong for Emmy when she came back to him, she cajoled; although she was not at all sure herself if that would ever happen. Marge or Ken would call, if there was any kind of a change, she assured him. And so, slowly, Clay had started to resume his normal daily activities, even though he had no heart in researching or writing his book.

Ivy had passed Clay's news on to Jack, Rob, and Paul. Texts and phone calls came in regularly to check up on him and Emmy, the woman they had never met. Clay was surrounded in love, but could see none of it. He was empty – except for the anguish he felt about Emmy.

The days marched on and turned into autumn. Clay was in the same zombie-like state he had been since he had first been told about Emmy's accident. Sitting on his patio, in the October sunshine, he stared out at the calm blue lake and reminisced about his time with Emmy. He had actually only known her for such a short time. It had been an idyllic summer, the walks along the pier and channel; the outings to the farmer's market for fresh vegetables, after which they would come home to cook together, the trips to the library or downtown for drinks at one of the local pubs, and of course, the road trip to Ludington to Father Marquette's memorial marker. He had been extremely attracted to Emmy the days before their trip, but on that day he had truly fallen in love. And then there was the afternoon on the Sapphire C, a day he would hold in his memory for the rest of his life. He remembered the gentle rocking, as the waves hit the hull. He remembered the sun warming their skin. He could clearly see Emmy in her brightly colored bikini, which accented the contours of her gorgeous body. His heart began to pound as he recalled the very moment he placed the bracelet on her arm and how their passion had consumed them. When his emotions overcame him, he went upstairs to his room. Clay cried in the shower where he thought no one could hear him, but he had no idea how loud his sobs were. Rachel, Clay's housekeeper, who was cleaning on the second floor, heard his wails, and cried with him. She stopped what she was doing and said a prayer for Emmy's health, and she also asked God to give Clay strength to face whatever was to come.

When Clay came out of his tear-filled agony, he suddenly became aware of one thing: he needed to ask Marge for the list that Emmy had about her family line. He thought if he held it in his hands, he could call upon past generations of gypsy princesses to help him. It was a ridiculous idea, and he knew it, but he was desperate. And then he recalled that Emmy had kept this list a secret from Marge and the rest of her family. He would have to make up a lie to cover for what he really wanted. He would say he wanted to ask permission to go into Emmy's room to look for a favorite book that he would like to read to her. So that's exactly what he did. He approached Marge at the hospital, and in a daze, caused by lack of sleep, she agreed that Clay could go through Emmy's room to look for the 'special' book.

"But Clay, I have something to tell you first."

"What is it? Is Emmy worse?"

"No, that's the problem," said Marge. "There's no change at all. The doctors want to take her off the ventilator."

"NO! She'll die, won't she?"

"Not necessarily. They want to give it a test run, to see if she can breathe on her own. The test will be closely monitored, and they have assured us, if she still needs the machine, she will be put back on it immediately. I wanted to tell you, because you might want to be here when they do it."

"Yes, yes, I do. When?" Fear choked his voice and when he spoke, it came out as a raspy squeak.

"Later today. We're waiting for Ken to show up, and then the doctor will come after he's out of surgery. Ken and I are allowed to be around the bed, but because you're not family, you won't. I'm sorry. Only two people can be in the room, or I would lie about your connection. But I need Ken with me, or I won't be able to handle it if anything goes wrong." Marge truly looked remorseful. No matter what Emmy thought of her sister, it was obvious that Marge did love her and cared about her well-being.

"I understand. Can I run home and catch Ken before he leaves? That way he can let me in the house."

"Sure. I'll call and tell him to wait for you. And thank you for loving Emmy, Clay. I mean it. She is a lucky woman."

Clay hugged Marge and thanked her in return for allowing him to be at the hospital with them, and then he ran off to meet Ken at the house. He needed to get that list.

∞

Ken greeted Clay at the door. He seemed anxious and afraid, his face was drawn and pasty white.

"I'm glad you made it so quickly, Clay," he said. "Come in. Marge just called again. The doctor will be in soon. I have to leave. I don't want Marge to go through this alone. Look around Emmy's room all you want, but lock up when you're gone. I already took care of Tessie's needs."

"Thank you, Ken, I really appreciate this. I pray that she is still alive when I get back."

"Don't drive carelessly. She'll need you, Clay, when she wakes up, and I'm sure she will."

Clay could see in Ken's eyes that he was not too sure of what he was saying. It was just meant to calm Clay down. As soon as Ken closed the door, Clay took a few minutes to pet Tessie. She seemed lonely and lost without the attention she was so used to. But after a few tussles of Tessie's fur, he ran up the steps. He had never been on the second floor of the Thompsons' house and had no idea what room was Emmy's, but a quick look into doorways and he soon found the correct room. Books were standing in a tower next to her bed, but otherwise it was neat and tidy. A little too neat. Her closet was empty, all signs of Emmy ever living there was gone. The top of the dresser had been cleaned of personal items, as was the bathroom. Clay's heart sank. It was a sign that when she left, she had no intention of coming back. For whatever reason Clay did not understand, she had been fleeing from him. Not expecting to find anything else, he opened a few drawers anyway, most were empty, but soon he came upon a small box in the nightstand. It was covered in a red silk with a Chinese pattern of egrets and herons. He tugged on the tassel pull, and when he opened it he was rewarded with a few sparks. The sapphire and diamond bracelet was inside. Clay wept when he saw it. Why would she leave it behind? Had their love meant nothing to her? The sparks were weak as if the bracelet was dying, too. He held it a moment to see if he could charge it back to life, but it was limp and cold, just as she was. A few other keepsakes were scattered loosely in the box. He pushed a few of them around, wanting to touch what had been important to her at one time. Then he noticed the yellowed paper stuck to the bottom of the box. That was it! Just what he was looking for. When he opened it up, the paper crackled with age. He read the names and dates. If this was accurate, it took her gypsy line back to 1820.

Clay put the paper and the bracelet back and took the entire box with him. As he ran toward the stairs, he realized that Tessie was trying to keep up with him. She must have been with him in Emmy's room all along, and he had not even noticed. He scooped her up with one arm and carried her down the steps, then after a quick cuddle, he put her down and locked the door. It was lucky he was not stopped by the police, because Clay broke every speed limit on the way. When he finally arrived at the hospital, no one was in the waiting room, so he inquired at the desk as to where the family was. The nurse told him they were already at Emmy's bedside, and the doctor was beginning to remove the ventilator.

Knowing he was not allowed in that room, he went back to the family lounge and waited. He sat down and said a prayer to God asking to save the woman he loved.

With his head bowed and his folded hands on his knees, he was unaware that he was not alone. He opened his eyes when he felt a hand gently pat his back. He looked up with tears in his eyes, and was surprised to see a group of people. He stood and hugged his best friends one at a time. Georgy and Jack, Rob and Rosie, Paul and Connie, and Ivy and Fox. The entire bunch had come to be his support. He was so happy to see them. He was ashamed that he had not told them about what he was going through sooner, but Ivy had made sure everyone knew. And when she had called to check up on Emmy, she asked to speak to Marge and was told what was about to happen. She had put out a 9-1-1 call, and every single person had responded.

"I can't believe you guys are here," said Clay, as he wiped tears from his eyes.

"Of course we would be, man. Everyone was there for me when I had my kidney transplant," answered Rob.

One look at Clay, and Jack could see Clay's devastation and fear. "We were not about to let you go through this all alone. We'll always be here for you, bro; no matter what. Even if you're not blood, we're family."

"Thanks, guys. And thank you, Ivy. It was so thoughtful of you to call everyone. If Emmy doesn't make it, I..." Clay stopped, unable to go any further.

Ivy wrapped her arms around the tall man and let him cry on her shoulder, as Fox gave him a manly pat on the back.

A few moments later, Marge came into the room. She was surprised at the amount of people who were there.

"What is it? Is she okay?" asked Clay, he couldn't tell a thing by looking at her face.

Marge sighed. "Good news and bad news. She's off the ventilator, and she is breathing on her own."

"That's wonderful," said several in the group.

"Well, yes and no. She is breathing on her own, but she is still in the coma."

Clay's face fell. "How long before she comes out of it?"

"I'm sorry, Clay. There's no answer to that. The doctor stressed that she could come out of it soon, or she might remain in this state forever. There's no swelling left in the brain and no apparent reason for the coma. Sometimes this just happens with a brain injury."

"What do we do? Just wait for her to die?"

"No, I'm not saying that. We'll be moving her to a rehab facility. They'll try some different tests that might be able to reach her."

"Can I see her?"

"Yes, you can go in now, but only you. I assume these are your friends, and therefore hers, too?"

"Oh, sorry Marge These are all of my friends. Emmy has never met them. I believe you may already know Fox Marzetti."

"Oh, yes, of course. I thought you looked familiar. You did the inspection on our house. How are you?"

"I'm fine, thank you. I'm sorry to hear about your sister. Clay tells us she is a lovely woman. Let me introduce you to our gang, here. This is my wife, Ivy and our sons Jack and Rob, and their respective ladies,

Georgy and Rosie. And these are our friends, Paul and Connie."

"Nice to meet all of you. Thank you for coming. I'm sure Clay appreciates it. Oh, here's Ken, he went for coffee, but unfortunately he didn't know there were others here, or he would have brought more. Sorry."

Marge explained to Ken who everyone was, and once the introductions were over, since Clay was no longer alone, and they had heard the results of the test, the group decided it was best to leave. The family lounge was getting quite crowded. As they said their goodbyes, Clay whispered to Ivy that he would like another meeting with her concerning what they had discussed last.

"Of, course. Call me when you get a break. I'm going home now to the kids, but Fox has a job to get to. I'm free all afternoon, if you want to come over."

"I'll be there. I'll text when I'm on my way. Thank you." He kissed her on the cheek, then he turned and headed toward Emmy's room, so he could see her before they began to transport her to the new facility.

She was still the same, but it was so much nicer to see her without all of the machines hooked up to her. Clay thought he detected a little more color to her complexion, but soon realized he had been deceiving himself. He touched her, stroked her hair, and kissed her. He talked lovingly to her, reminding her of things only the two of them knew, but nothing brought even a flicker to her eye.

"Emmy, can you hear me? Emmy? I love you so much. We've just found each other. Don't leave me now. I'll wait until you're ready to come back. I'll wait as long as it takes. There will never be another for me. You belong to me, Emmy. You're mine. You're all I want." Then he sobbed more tears.

Chapter Twenty-four

The hospital was a strange place. Some people came with flowers and gifts; they came to visit loved ones in groups or alone. Sometimes they were laughing in the hallway or in the cafeteria. Clay could only assume it was because of a birth of a new baby or a successful surgery which had relieved all those who worried. But then in the midst of those people, Clay would see a loner like himself, sad and dejected, looking like they had the weight of the world on their shoulders. Once he almost approached a man, but the thought of trying to help someone in their despair when he was in his own was too much to bear. He felt guilty for not doing something. Maybe he should have tried to be there for the other man. Maybe it would have helped, but maybe he would have been intruding on his privacy. It was a thin line, and he had not known what to do, so he had done nothing.

Today as he walked to his car, with his head hanging low and his shoulders slumped, he was not aware of the woman who was following him. She was old and wrinkled. Her clothing was faded and mismatched, and she carried a heavy bag, that almost dragged on the ground. When Clay got to his car, and struggled to find his keys, she walked up to him. He jumped when he heard, "Bad day?"

"Yes, yes, it was, I'm afraid. But then they all have been for a while." She looked homeless, or at the very least very poor; perhaps she was looking for some money, he thought. She smiled when he talked to her, showing yellowed teeth. He had a sense that he already knew her, but he saw nothing familiar in her face.

"Just do what you know you have to. It will all work out the way it was meant to," she whispered.

"What? What was that?" Clay looked into her eyes, and a chill ran through him.

"Never fear. You're doing well. You're taking care of her like you should. I thank you. *She belongs to me, and therefore I belong to you.*" She nodded towards him, then touched his arm.

Suddenly, Clay's vision became blurry, and he felt faint. He leaned back onto his car to steady himself. He shook his head and ran his hands over his eyes to clear them, but when he looked again, she was gone. He spun around the parking lot, looking for a sign of her, but there was no one nearby. No other car door slammed shut, and no motor revved up. He was alone. She had vanished.

∞

Clay arrived at Fox and Ivy's house a shaken man, his face pale, and his brow laced with drops of perspiration. Ivy could tell something had happened the moment she opened the door. She brought him inside and gave him a warm cup of tea.

"Clay, what happened?" she asked.

Before Clay had a chance to answer, two children came running out to see him. Sal and Ruby had always been attracted to the tall man with the strange way of talking. When Clay saw them he smiled his first big smile in a long time. The kids talked about their newest toys and showed him pages they had recently colored. Finally, Ivy sent them off to play in their rooms.

"Sorry, Clay. Things are always quite hectic here. Sal is going to be picked up by my friend soon for a play date with her kids. And Ruby will be going down for a nap. Let's drink our tea and chat, and when things are settled we can have a real talk. So, how are you really doing?"

The two talked about writing and research, about historical places and people in the West Michigan area, and the ups and downs of the publishing world. They talked about anything but the reason he was there. It wasn't long before there was a knock on the door, and when Ivy opened it a little boy was standing there, waiting excitedly for his friend. He said meekly, "Is Sal ready to go?"

Ivy turned and called, "Sal, they're here. Don't forget your jacket. It's getting cooler out. Hurry. Your friends are waiting." She kissed her son, and waved at the mom waiting outside in the car. Then she turned to Clay. "Will you give me a moment to settle Ruby down?"

When Ivy left the room, Clay reached in his shirt pocket and retrieved the piece of paper with Emmy's list of names. Thinking of what had happened in the parking lot, caused his hands to shake all over again. He pulled out his phone, glanced at the time, and then he called London.

"Mr. Blythe, so glad I caught you. Clay – um Michael Harris, here. Sorry, I know it's late, but I have a favor to ask of you." Then he proceeded to give Mr. Blythe instructions as to how to find the fortunetelling shop. He asked him to question Gina on a few things.

He thought a formal visit would get better results than a phone conversation from the States.

"What do you need to know, Mr. Harris?"

"Tell her who you're there for and ask her what this phrase means. Just say, *'she belongs to me and therefore I belong to you.'* Can you do that for me? You must say it word for word. Did you get it?"

"Of course, Mr. Harris. I'll get on it tomorrow, and I'll call when I have something for you."

"Thank you, Mr. Blythe. I'll be waiting for your call." Clay hung up just as Ivy tiptoed out of Ruby's room.

"Success," she whispered. "She's down for the count. We have about two hours. Now, let's talk about why you're really here. What's up?"

"I'm not sure where to start; it's all so confusing."

"Start at the beginning, as they say."

"Well, I've already told you a little bit. Now I need to question you more about your books."

"About what, Clay?"

"About the necklace, the gypsies, all of it, I guess."

271

"Why is it so important to you?" asked Ivy, cautiously. She had never shared anything about the magic of her necklace with anyone. Her third cousin knew of its existence as well as her best friend, because of old photos and stories they had discovered together, but they had no idea of the extent of its powers. Ivy had promised Fox never to reveal anything about their secret.

"I'm embarrassed to say it out loud. It sounds so weird." He sucked in his breath and proceeded cautiously with his tale. Clay told Ivy how he had finally offered the bracelet to Emmy as a test to see how it reacted to being on her arm. His wistful smile and slight blush told Ivy everything she needed to know. He was deeply in love and the bracelet had brought passion to the couple beyond belief in the same way that the ruby and diamond necklace had worked for her and Fox and others before them. "I'm thrilled for you, Clay. I can see your love has been cemented for all time."

"But that's just it. On the day we – uh, 'used' the bracelet," said Clay, with embarrassment, "we told each other private things. Emmy shared with me something she had never tells anyone. I don't think, in this case, she would mind if I told you. Emmy has visions, mostly about people. She tries to hide it, because it scares people off. I think she had a vision she did not want me to know about, and that's why she left me."

"She left you?"

"Yes, I'm afraid she saw something about me she didn't like. Apparently, she was leaving me when the accident happened. Her closet is empty. She only left the bracelet behind and a list."

"Why do you think she left the bracelet?"

"I think it represents our love and for some reason she couldn't face it." With those words, Clay struggled to keep his composure. Ivy watched as his jaw bone clenched several times. He looked down at what he was holding in his hands. "And she left this." He handed it to Ivy.

"It looks old. What is it?"

"It's the list of names she told me about when we were on the boat. A list her grandmother gave to her and

273

told her to keep secret. I feel terrible violating her privacy, but I have no choice. I have to find a way to reach her."

Ivy began to read, and as she did so, she could see it was a genealogy of ancestors.

Emmaline Regina Simmons – Gypsy Princess.

She pointed to the first name. "Is this Emmy?"

"Yes, it is, and then it goes back through her family line."

Naomi Regina (Queenie) Holmes Simmons -- Emmy's mother

Kezia Regina White Holmes – Emmy's grandmother

Regina Sorenson White – great-grandmother

Yana Regina Andrushkev Sorenson (1895) – 2x grandmother, and her sister Yulia Regina Andrushkev Karpenko (1900)

Regina also known as Gina (1879) Ukraine – 3x great-grandmother

Gina (1860) Ukraine – 4x great-grandmother

Gina (1845) Ukraine – 5x great-grandmother

Gina (1820) Ukraine – 6x great-grandmother, lover to Stas Karpenko, King of the Gypsies, but never married.

And as she neared the bottom of the list, she turned white with shock. Gina, Gina, Gina, all the way back to 1820. Ivy looked at Clay, started to talk, but her mouth opened and no words came out.

"But – but – this means..."

"What does it mean, Ivy? Tell me, please."

"It means that the first Gina shown here in 1820 was meant to marry Stas Karpenko, who is Fox's earliest known Gypsy ancestor. And the next Gina was the one who thwarted the marriage of Bo and Anya, which disrupted a family line. Anya is on *my* family tree. Yes, Clay, it's all real. A Gina did come to me and tell me that she was trying to right the wrongs of the past. She said

Fox and I would bring everything back into alignment when we got together, and that's why the necklace was meant for us."

"How does that work for me and Emmy, then?"

"Well, we have Emmy's complete line right here. She is part of the same Gypsy camp and is truly a gypsy princess. That might explain the visions. It seems she has inherited some fortunetelling tendencies. But I'm not sure why the bracelet is trying to bring you two together."

Clay thought a moment, and then added, "Here's another strange fact. I have a detective working in London for me. He's been trying to convince my birth mother to keep in touch with me, but all she has said so far, is that she does know her rapist's name. He was a friend of the family and an older man. His name is Artem Karpenko. When I heard that last name, I knew I had read about it in your books. It's one of the reasons, as well as how the bracelet reacts, as to why I have been questioning you."

"You're kidding! Karpenko? But that would mean that somehow you are connected to Fox's line, too. That branch is off his mother's line. *Anton* Karpenko, is a descendant of Bo, of Anya and Bo fame. Yulia Andrushkev is on Gina's line. Anton and Yulia are Fox's great-grandparents. Somehow you are also connected to Stas, the Gypsy King."

"Do you think that's possible? Do I have gypsy blood, also?"

Ivy took Clay's hands in hers. "I think for whatever reason, this jewelry only works for those in this particular clan, and only for those who are meant to be together. I'll see if I can track anything back on that name, although it will be difficult since you are illegitimate and adopted, and we have nothing other than your birth father's name. But Clay, I can almost promise you, you are part of our family. Welcome." Then they hugged in joy as their hearts soared at the new family connection; Ivy laughed when the baby within her rounded belly kicked at the same time. Even the baby

277

was happy to meet a new family member, however distant on the family tree.

"I can't wait to tell Fox," said Ivy, wiping away tears. Now she understood why she had felt so connected to Clay, who was called Michael then, when she first met him, and why he had reminded her so much of her husband. The genes were strong. The Karpenko men were all so very handsome, tall and dark. "I'm going to dig right into your family tree and see what I can come up with. I love a good challenge."

"Thank you so much. I'm going back home for a bit and wait for news of when and where Emmy is being moved, and then I'm going to read her this list of names, and see if it stirs up any kind of emotion. I'm going to try to call upon her gypsy grandmothers' spirits. You've given me hope, Ivy. I can never thank you enough for trusting me and sharing with me about the necklace. It really means a lot. And I promise to never tell a single soul, other than Emmy, of course."

As Clay was driving home, he went over and over everything Ivy and he had discussed. It still sounded crazy, as it would to any sane person, but where Emmy was concerned nothing was impossible, and now he had something to hope for. He was going to make it happen. He would bring her back one way or another.

Chapter Twenty-five

Moving Emmy to a new place had not happened as quickly as Clay had thought it would. Marge and Ken were insistent on placing her in a good facility that specialized in coma patients, and one that was close to home. There were only two that met their requirements, and there were no beds available. They had to keep Emmy in the hospital a full week longer while they waited for an opening. Clay had tried to read the list to Emmy in the hospital, but every time he was about to do it, a nurse or Marge or Ken would come in. If he had been reading her a story, it would not have been a problem, but he did not want to get caught with the list, since Marge knew nothing about it. According to what Emmy had told him, Marge did not have the same abilities to see the future that she did. And she also knew there had always been jealousy with the closeness Emmy and her grandmother had shared. Clay was not about to rock the 'sister' boat at this stage.

While Clay was waiting, he received a call from Mr. Blythe on the other side of the ocean. Mr. Blythe informed him that they had set about trying to track down Gina and the fortunetelling shop just as Clay had described. Clay still had the business card she had given him, so on a previous call, he had read the address that was shown there to Mr. Blythe. But neither Mr. Blythe himself nor any of his staff had been able to find it. As a matter of fact, he said, in order to double-check what his staff had told him, he had gone there himself, and he was standing on the exact spot where the shop should be right now, and there was nothing there. It was just an old warehouse with a solid brick wall. It was obvious that there had never been a shop of any kind there, at least not for many, many years. There was no plate glass window with colorful scarves or an exotic door with a bell. There was not even an entrance to the building on this side of the road. Yes, the street was brick, but that was the only thing that looked anything like what Clay had told them to look for. It was a real puzzle. Knowing how insistent Clay had been that this was the place, Mr. Blythe's staff had delved into old property records for land sales and taxes. No shop of any kind had ever been in this location. It had always been a warehouse district.

Clay thanked Mr. Blythe and then asked if he had any more news from his biological mother. There was a sigh and then an apology. Mr. Blythe said Mrs. McMurtry had asked not to contact her ever again. She felt her husband had been getting suspicious of her behavior, and she had no intention of ever letting him know anything about her past. Mr. Blythe strongly urged that Clay let his quest rest, and Clay reluctantly agreed. He had never meant to cause Fiona any pain or anguish, and if it was reaching that point, it was time to back down. At least he had been able to discover his father's name. Whether that was a good or bad thing was yet to be determined.

During Clay's time away from Emmy, he tried to keep busy by continuing his research on Father Marquette. There were so many books to read and facts to get in order before he was actually ready to put words 'down on paper,' so to speak. But eventually, it all began to come together. Clay now felt like he really knew the man who had befriended so many Native Americans. Because of his efforts for his church in converting men and women to Christianity, many souls had been saved. And if not for his ability to make friends and be accepted among them, Michigan might have fallen into other foreign hands, because there was a struggle for years to come between the British and the French. Mackinac Island in particular was caught in the tug of war between the two European countries. Each country recognized the importance of owning the heavily wooded area with all of the lakes and rivers, as well as the seaway connection between the Great Lakes. Years later Mackinac Island would be strongly held by the British as many battles were fought there, while others tried to gain control.

Clay rubbed his eyes. Working on his Father Marquette project took his mind off of Emmy for a short while, but worry was always present. What if she never came out of it? What if she did and she was paralyzed? What if she didn't know him anymore? What if she remained in a coma for the rest of her life? She was completely off of life support now except for a feeding tube. Would Marge and Ken finally decide to remove her last bit of life sustaining nourishment? The love of his life could remain like this forever. Her beauty was still obvious, but she was frail. Blue veins now showed through her translucent skin. It looked like her life was slipping away. The Thompsons held all the power to call an end to it, and Clay realized he was in no position to have a say. He was not her husband; therefore he had no rights. Perhaps it would be best if Emmy just passed away in her sleep, then no one would have to make the horrible decision. It was too early to make these choices, but Clay had no doubt, that late at night in the dark in the Thompsons' bedroom, some of these very thoughts were whispered. He put his head on his desk and cried out as he begged God to hear his prayer.

∞

When the day finally came that Emmy was to be moved to a new facility, the Thompsons and Clay were there to watch as her still body was loaded into a transport van. She looked so white, her long dark hair tied up in a bun to keep it out of her face and off her neck. They had crossed her hands over her abdomen, so to Clay she looked like she had already passed away. He had tried to choke back the sobs, but they could no longer be stilled. He was embarrassed for his show of emotion, until he looked at Marge. She had tears streaming down her cheeks, also. Ken was the stoic one; he stood with a straight back and a somber look on his face. He was a rock for them both.

The staff had asked that they give them a few hours to get her settled in at the new facility before they came to visit, and they had decided to respect their wishes. Ken asked Clay if he would like to join them for lunch at their home. They needed to be there for a bit for Tessie. She was very confused, Ken said, with all of the comings and goings of the last few months. She was not used to being left alone for such long periods. Clay agreed to meet them at the house in about a half hour.

After freshening up a bit, Clay walked next door. Ken met him at the door with a small smile. "Come in, Clay. I'm sorry our first neighborly visit had to be under such awful circumstances."

"Yes, me too. I should have come over as soon as I moved in to introduce myself."

"I believe the fault is on our side. You were new, and we should have welcomed you to the neighborhood, but we were busy getting ready to leave for our vacation. It was a hectic time. I apologize."

"No problem," said Clay.

Marge heard the voices and came to the door to greet Clay. "Hello Clay, come in. I take it you've already been in our home?" She raised an eyebrow, wondering exactly what had gone on in her house while they were on their cruise of the Aegean Sea.

"No, I have not, actually. Well, except for a few times when we ate together on the patio, and the other day when I came to get that book."

"Oh, yes. The book. Did you find it? I never saw you reading to her."

"No, I did not find it. It might have been a library book that she already returned," lied Clay.

Marge clicked her tongue. "Emmy was always such a reader. I never cared much for books. She loved spending her time all alone, lost in another world. Daddy used to get so angry at her when she would be late with a library book and had to pay a fine. Maybe that's why I didn't read. That way he had no reason to be angry with me." Marge laughed. "Daddy and I had a special bond, and I didn't want to do anything to break it, I guess."

"Clay, would you care for anything to drink?" asked Ken.

"Just some iced tea, if you have it," responded Clay.

"I'm sure we do; we always have some on hand, but let me check. We haven't been able to keep up with things like we usually do. Give me a minute."

"If you don't have any, water is fine."

Marge sat down and gestured for Clay to do the same. "Now, tell me about how you met Emmy. We haven't had a chance to really get to know each other. There's been too much drama."

Clay stiffened at the word 'drama.' Was Marge reverting to her old criticisms and jealousies of Emmy? In Clay's opinion, what Emmy was going through was not drama. It was terrifying and emotional and exhausting. Emmy had not brought this on herself. What was Marge implying?

Marge studied Clay a moment, while licking her lips and patting her hair in a flirtatious way. "Don't tell me my Emmy came on to you?"

Clay offered her a tight smile. "Not at all. We actually met at the channel when we were both on walks. We didn't even know we were neighbors for quite a while. We bumped into each other again at the farmer's market, and struck up a conversation. Then from that meeting we began to see each other more regularly. There wasn't too much to it, really." Clay was not about to tell Marge all of the details about how he spied on his neighbor and fell in love without ever seeing her face. Some things were better left unsaid.

"Yes, Emmy has a way of pulling men in. Beware, she is a charmer, but it won't last. She gets bored and always moves on to someone new."

"Marge! I thought we talked about this," said Ken sharply, as he returned with their glasses of tea. Ice clinked against the side of the glasses as he walked, sounding like a wind chime and taking some of the sting out of his rebuke. Marge hung her head for a bit. It was obvious her husband had the upper hand in the marriage. "Besides, she was with Daniel for years. You make it sound like she had a new man every other week."

"Sorry, I didn't mean it the way it came out. It's just that Emmy is different than most girls. She's quiet and introspective. Men seemed to be drawn to her. Maybe it's because she is so mysterious, with her dark foreign look. I know you're in love with her, Clay. But I'm just saying you should be wary. Things aren't always what they seem. Emmy has secrets that she is not willing to share. I only hope you never find out whatever they are. She can be dangerous."

"Marge!" said Ken sharply.

Clay leaned forward and looked Marge right in the eye. "I hope I do find out all of her secrets, because that will mean that she has come back to us. I know plenty about Emmy, and now I know one thing for sure. You have not always been her best advocate. I thought Emmy was wrong when she told me what you thought of her and how you treated her, because you have been nothing but wonderful since she went into the hospital. But today I am seeing the side of you she has told me about. You are jealous and spiteful. And of what?" Clay's voice rose to a higher pitch, as he stood to go. "She is lying in a bed, hanging between life and death. She is living in a world that could be dark and scary, and you have not said one good thing about her since I arrived. I'll be having my lunch somewhere else today, thank you." And with that, Clay stomped out of the room and slammed the door behind him. All he heard as he walked away was Ken saying, "Marge, how could you?"

When Clay got home, he was shaking with rage. Everything Emmy had first told him about Marge was true. Yes, she had shown worry and tears for her sister, but looking back, Clay now wondered how much of it had been an act. He could see now that there really was no love lost between the two and probably never would be. If this traumatic event had not brought Marge closer to Emmy, then nothing would.

Clay glanced at the clock on his phone. It was way past the hour that the staff at Emmy's new residence had requested he wait. Clay decided to skip lunch and head back. He needed to be alone with Emmy for a few minutes, and he was not in a mood to see Marge again today.

Chapter Twenty-six

The new facility smelled like a mixture of floral room deodorizing scent and pine cleaning supplies. Although not unpleasant, it was not an odor one would want to smell every day. Clay wondered how the staff was able to tolerate it. Maybe after working here for so long, their noses had become accustomed to the mixed fragrances, much like how someone who works in a bakery no longer smells the baked bread and fried donuts.

The girl at the front desk was pleasant enough. She asked him to sign the register, pointed him to Emmy's room, and reminded him to sign out when he left. He walked down one hall, turned left, took a few steps before turning right, and then he entered her room which was on the right. She was alone and looked exactly the same as she had in the hospital. Except for her surroundings, nothing had changed. The large vase of sunflowers he had sent had preceded his arrival. He moved them slightly so she would have a good view of them when she woke up, because he was positive she would wake when he began to read. He kissed her lightly on the lips while caressing her fingers. There was no response, as usual.

Clay pulled his chair closer to the bed, eager to talk to Emmy, hoping that she would hear his voice and have some kind of reaction.

"Emmy, my love, I'm here. You're not alone. We have been taking very good care of you while we wait for you to come back to us. I'm sure that won't be long now, because I thought of something you might like to hear, and I want to read it to you. Is that okay?"

Clay paused a moment, as he waited for the response he feared might not come, and when it didn't, he pulled out the old piece of paper from his pocket. He listened to see if echoing footsteps on the tiled floor announced that someone was coming, but he heard no one in the halls.

"Remember when you told me what your grandmother had given you? The list? Remember that? Well, I brought it with me today. I want to remind you of your heritage, and what a fine one it is. You have a reason to live. You are truly a princess; royal blood runs through your veins. Do you need to be reminded of how that works? Let me tell you. This is how it goes:

Emmaline Regina Simmons – Gypsy Princess

Naomi Regina (Queenie) Holmes Simmons -- Emmy's mother

Kezia Regina White Holmes – Emmy's grandmother

Regina Sorenson White – great-grandmother

Yana Regina Andrushkev Sorenson (1895) – 2x great-grandmother, and her sister Yulia Regina Andrushkev Karpenko (1900)

Regina also known as Gina (1879) Ukraine – 3x great-grandmother

Gina (1860) Ukraine – 4x great-grandmother

Gina (1845) Ukraine – 5x great-grandmother

Gina (1820) Ukraine – 6x great-grandmother, lover to Stas Karpenko, King of the Gypsies, but never married.

"Now, Emmy according to this and according to what I have discovered, you are from a gypsy tribe in Ukraine. What your grandmother told you was all true." Clay paused to wipe some tears off of his cheek. "The reason I know this is because I have discussed it with Ivy. I hope you're okay with that. The reason I talked to her about it is because her husband Fox's line is of the same lineage as yours. Fox's great-grandmother, Yulia, and your great-great-grandmother, Yana, were sisters. I guess you are cousins in some way. Here's where it gets complicated, Emmy. Stay with me, okay? Fox's great-

grandfather's name was Anton Karpenko, and he connects back to the same Stas Karpenko mentioned in your list. I can't prove it, Emmy, but I think your Gina from the 1820s was meant to marry Stas and somehow that union was blocked. I believe your Gina had Stas' baby, but she was not able to marry him or chose not to, and that child's birth began another gypsy line. I think that Gina is still trying to put that right, because I have discovered that my father's last name is Karpenko — Artem Karpenko, actually. We are meant to be together, Emmy. You and I. Do you see that? That's why you can't leave me. Gina wants us to be together. Do you hear me? You truly are a princess. Let me tell you about it once again."

And Clay began to read the list over and over. It became like a chant. Each time he finished, he looked to see if there was any sign of recognition, anything at all. But Emmy remained in a deep slumber. With a heavy heart Clay kissed Emmy with more pressure on her lips, hoping to stir something within her. But still there was nothing. He breathed a heavy sigh and left. Placing one foot after another, he slowly walked to his car. He never saw the movement under her eyelids after he left the room.

∞

Emmaline Regina, also known simply as Gina, seemed surprised to find herself in the gypsy camp. She did not remember coming here after bathing in the stream where she and Stas always met. She looked down at her clothing. Something was wrong. This skirt did not belong to her, did it? It was so colorful. Beautiful, but not at all what she usually wore. But when she thought hard about it, she remembered it was the very skirt she had hiked up to her ankles when she first went wading. She touched her neck and felt heavy ropes of beads and chains. Her hand rose to her hair where she discovered a braid hanging on the side over her shoulder; it was woven with a ribbon. How did that get there? Gina felt a pain and rubbed her forehead. She felt so out of place, as if she had never been here before. But these were her people. She knew them all by name, especially the one she wished she could forget. Her name was Olnya, the tramp who was betrothed to Stas.

Stas was Gina's beloved. They had known each other since they were children, as had Olnya. There had always been a rivalry between the two girls. Both were equally beautiful in their own right, but Olnya was the daughter of Stas' father's best friend. And Stas' father was King. So when the two men made a pact at the time of their children's birth, that they would betroth them when they were seven, and it had been set before the council, nothing could ever change that arrangement. The only problem was that Stas and Gina had fallen madly in love when they were fourteen. Even though it was a young love, it was very powerful. At first it was nothing more than child's play, teasing and kissing in the bushes. But within a year they had advanced toward stronger desires, as they began to explore each other with eager curiosity. Stas always wanted more, and Gina, against her mother's advice, had given it to him -- whatever he wanted and whenever he wanted it. Of course, her mother knew nothing about the bracelet he brought to her one day when he was fifteen.

Gina glanced at her bare wrist as she walked across the camp to her tent. How she wished she still had it on. Her body ached to own it. It was so beautiful the way it flashed and sent sparks over them as they made love. But Stas always took it back when they were done with their lovemaking. He said it actually belonged to the royal family. He said soon it would be his, when later this year he turned sixteen. Then he would be able to use it whenever he wanted to, and he would not have to return it. It was his right of passage to use the bracelet for true love, and to produce heirs. Gina questioned him if he had ever used it with Olnya. She was furious when Stas answered yes. They fought for the first time, arguing loudly, and Gina had even beat him with her fists, pummeling his chest in a jealous rage. But when he had assured her it had not worked, Gina relented a little, and begged him never to try it again on Olnya. He promised he would not, because he said it was obvious the passion it produced was reserved for her alone, and she had believed him.

Gina threw back the opening to her tent with anger, as she thought about Olnya and Stas lying together in the grass, as she had with him. Life was cruel. She was meant for Stas, no one else! He had told her so many times. He said she belonged to him. She needed to get that bracelet, so she could control when they used it. Maybe then Stas would ask his parents if he could marry her instead. It was not against the rules, but his father was the only one who could go to the council and ask to annul the betrothal. Of course, that was usually done only when there was a falling out between the fathers, and as far as Gina knew, the men were still as tight as brothers.

Gina suddenly felt lightheaded. She had a terrible headache, and she was so tired she could not keep her eyes open. She laid down on her pallet, and instantly fell into a restless sleep. She dreamed of sapphires and diamonds and a passion beyond compare. But when

she saw a flash of rubies, her heart ached, and she cried
in her sleep.

∞

Emmy's rapid eye movement was picking up speed. Stas -- she wanted Stas. No, Clay -- she wanted Clay. She was so confused. Where was she? Why was she here? The smell of smoking goat turning on the spit made her mouth water. The tinkle of wind chimes caused her to turn her head slightly to the left and then back. The sound of the men playing their instruments around the fire beckoned her to join in and sing. She turned around and around as names of women filled her head, names that meant nothing to her except her own. She tried to call out to Clay, but no sound left her mouth. Why was she trying to call Clay? She was meant for Stas; she had always known that. She wanted Clay so badly, she needed him, he would explain her confusion, but she must stay here. It was where she belonged. The camp was her home. And there was still a chance Stas would marry her, especially now that she was to have his baby.

Chapter Twenty-seven

The phone was buzzing on his nightstand. It took a moment for Clay to clear his head, but as soon as he saw that the number calling him was the rehab facility, he was instantly wide awake.

"Hello?"

"Hello, Mr. Harris. This is Lifeline Rehab Facility. We thought you might want to know that Emmy has had some minor improvements. Her sister Marge asked me to call you, and keep you up to date."

Clay sat up and tried to pull on his pants while holding the phone at the same time. He finally hit the speaker button and continued to get dressed.

"What do you mean, there's been an improvement? What is happening? Is she awake?"

"No, it's nothing like that, yet. I'm sorry."

Clay's heart sank and he began to slow down his frantic movements. "What is it, then? Why did you call so early?"

"Our monitors alerted us that she has had some rapid eye movement, which means she is dreaming. She has come a little closer to the surface. This could continue for quite a while, or she could go back to the depth of sleep she was at before, *or* she could just come out of the coma when we least expect it."

"So there's no reason for me to get there quickly?"

"I'm sorry, there isn't. And I believe Mr. and Mrs. Thompson are on their way now. They will be meeting with the doctor soon, so you can get more updates from them. Due to HIPPA laws, you know, I won't be able to tell you anything else. I should not have told you as much as I did, since you are not a spouse or blood relative."

"Thank you for the call. I appreciate it." Clay hung up. He was both elated and disappointed at the same time. Clay assumed that at least the rapid eye movement meant she was trying to come out of the coma, but he was just making a guess. With his recent fallout with Marge, he would most certainly be left in the dark from now on. She had not even had the courtesy to call him herself, but instead had asked the facility to do it.

Clay shook his head in disgust. He was determined not to let it get him down. He would continue with his visits to Emmy. He would just make sure that he was never at the rehab home whenever the Thompsons were there. Living next door to people you did not like or respect was not ideal, but it could be done, especially with his tall hedges. His long driveway took him back to his house through a wide expanse of lawn and trees. It's not like some houses that had their driveways side by side. It would be easy to avoid Emmy's family.

Knowing that the Thompsons were going to be there this morning was helpful. Clay could slow down his morning routine and arrive later, perhaps after lunch. He was eager to try his list reading therapy again. He was sure it was what had brought her to the REM sleep. He must have reached her at some level. If he kept it up, perhaps it would encourage her to come out of the coma.

The morning dragged on. Clay tried to work on his book, but his heart was not in it. He turned on TV, but all he found were silly shows of no interest. He clicked over to the news, but it was too stressful. After pouring himself another cup of coffee, he grabbed a book and went outside to read. The day was a little nippy, but he didn't mind. It was all part of the changing seasons. Looking out at the lake, everything seemed barren now. In his worry about Emmy, he had missed the beautiful changing colors as the trees went through their transformation. The leaves had all fallen now, lying brown and crispy on the ground. The bare branches of the trees formed a stark image against the gray sky, as if an artist had sketched the view in charcoal.

Clay had already put his large boat in dry dock, and a work crew he had hired pulled the smaller boat, the jet skis, and paddle boats onto land. Everything was covered with blue tarps, waiting for the snow and ice which would come soon enough. Somehow, Emmy had completely missed the fall season, and so had Clay. It had always been one of his favorite times of year, and he had been looking forward to sharing it with her. A trip to St. Ignace to see Father Marquette's final resting place had been on his mind. It would have been a beautiful drive for a color tour, but now that time has passed. Clay only hoped there would be a next year for him and Emmy. His face crumpled once again, as it often did. He ran his hand over his eyes, trying to block out the images of her lying in that bed, still and pale. He much preferred to recall her laughing on the boat – her body warm and responsive.

A little bark and a few yips brought Clay out of his thoughts. Tessie. She was outside, which meant the

Thompsons were home now. There would be no chance of him running into them today. Clay hurriedly went inside, grabbed his list of names, and drove back to the rehab home.

∞

He was at her side, studying her face. There was no sign of life there at all. He could see none of the eye movements they had told him about. She was so still. How was it possible to be alive and not move at all? Did she itch? Did she need to move an arm or leg for comfort? How did they know if she was too cold or hot? He was told she got massages and was rubbed down with lotion before they changed her body position to prevent bed sores, but he had not been here when that was done. She was always the same when he came. He kissed her first on the cheek, and then on the eyelids, willing them to move. He stood back and watched again for a few seconds, before placing a passionate kiss on her lips, but passion was only thrilling when it was returned. Her lips were sweet and soft, but very flaccid. He felt no response whatsoever.

Clay's face fell in despair, but he was void of all tears today. So with a big sigh, he began to read to her once more. Name after name, beginning to end, end to beginning, he recited Emmy's heritage, as his voice droned on.

∞

Gina woke in his arms. He had returned to her during the night. It was the first time he had ever come into her tent. They had always met in meadows and fields and the deep woods. "Stas," she murmured, stretching sensually, wrapping her arms around his neck. "You came. I dreamed of you; I yearned for you. I thought I heard you call my name. I heard Gina over and over. Was it you?"

"It wasn't me, my sweet. I just recently got here. I fear I jostled you when I crawled in next to you and my movements woke you."

"I don't care that you woke me," she said drowsily. "All that matters is that you are here. How did you sneak in without being seen? If Olnya sees you come in here, she will be furious."

"Yes, she will, but I have something to tell you, and it can't be held back any longer."

"Tell me, my love. Are you going to profess your love for me to the troupe? Are you finally going to make a choice and claim me? I already know how much you love me. You tell me often and show me more," she laughed, with a husky voice as she kissed his bare chest. "I can't wait for everyone else to know." Gina smiled in a sensuous and suggestive manner. "Shall we use the bracelet now? Did you bring it? I am so eager for your love, even without it; you know I can never get enough of you."

"I did bring the bracelet. Raise your arm and let me place it on."

Gina lifted her arm and Stas kissed it from her elbow to the palm of her hand, sending shivers to her very core. Then he place the sapphires on her wrist and hooked the clasp. Instantly, sparks began to fly, and the two lovers fell back in a frantic embrace. The powers seemed stronger than ever before. Gina cried out with her love for him, as he whispered in her ear. He was hers; all hers. She would be queen someday, and then she would be free to wear all the jewelry of the royal family. But once they were sated, and Stas was lying next to her, his skin still wet with exertion, she sensed something different in his demeanor.

"What is it, my darling? What do you need to tell me? You go first, because I have something to tell you, too," she smiled, mysteriously.

Stas took a deep breath. He was afraid of hurting her. He knew it would crush her, but it had to be said. "I need to say this uninterrupted. Will you abide by that?"

"Yes, anything, my sweet. Go ahead." Gina was afraid now. Something was wrong. She could see it in his face.

"I have been given an order by my father. I am to declare my love for Olnya. Time is running out for the formal proclamation of the wedding to come."

"No!"

"Now, you said you would not interrupt. Please, let me continue." He placed his fingers over her lips, and felt a single teardrop fall on his hand. "I have not used the bracelet on Olnya, because it does not work for her. It only brings passion to you and me. But there is another piece. It is the one my mother and father used to determine they were meant for each other. It is a ruby and diamond necklace, and it is meant to select the true queen, so that she may produce the rightful heir. So you see, even though this bracelet works for our passion, it is not meant to continue the family line."

"How can you say such a thing?" cried Gina, angrily.

"According to my father, if the ruby necklace vibrates for a woman, as it did for my mother when he placed it around her neck, then she is the one who was foretold many generations ago. I'm afraid to tell you, my lovely Gina, but the rubies were wonderful when I was with Olnya. It was incredible. Our lovemaking was more than I ever dreamed possible."

"More than what we have? More than what we just did? How could that be?"

Gina's voice began to rise to a level that would alert people nearby that she was in distress. Stas did not want anyone to barge in thinking they needed to save her from him.

"Shhh. You must keep quiet. No one outside the family knows of the existence of these jewels. I'm truly sorry; I have made love with Olnya on several occasions now, but until I used the necklace, I had no idea that she was meant for me. She is the one our forefathers have chosen."

"You promised me you would not tempt her again. How could you?" Gina was doubled over with her sobs, now. Her heart was breaking. It was clear that her Stas would never be hers to marry, but then she recalled she did have one card left to play. She lifted her head from her lap, and Stas saw her unhappy face change to fury. "You may have your Olnya, and you may make many children with her, but your first born will always belong to me!"

Stas was shocked at the change in her, and it took a moment for what she had said to sink in. "What are you telling me?"

"I am going to have your baby. I will make sure the whole camp knows who it belongs to. I will not be treated like someone to frolic with whenever you have an urge to satisfy. If you can't marry me, then you will at least acknowledge your daughter, for it is to be a girl. I have seen her in my visions. You will treat her with respect. You will give her this bracelet to pass on until it can right the wrong you have done to me this day. I will never forgive you, Stas. If you do not do what I am requesting, I will take you to the council."

Stas turned white. It would not do to have a stain on his good name right before he married, because it would follow him throughout his entire life, and he would lose respect when he became king. "I will do as

314

you say, but I must first go to my father with the request. He will make the final decision."

"No, I make the decision! There is no other option. You can tell him that for me. And I want my tent moved closer to yours. You may still want to visit on occasion, and I intend to be ready when you do. But I will no longer wear the bracelet for you. It belongs to my future daughter now, whose name will be Gina, like mine, and all to follow for all time."

Stas looked at her steadily for what seemed like an eternity, then he quietly rose to go to the King's tent. There was much to discuss.

Gina's head hurt. It hurt so much. She clutched it and moaned as she fell back onto the thick fur throw. She felt her baby kick and she passed out, and when she next opened her eyes, she was not sure where she was. She was in a tent, the same one she had dreamed about before. The thick bedding below her was unfamiliar. The cooking pans stacked up were made of iron, and the spoons were made of wood. There were jars of unfamiliar spices. Everything seemed so rustic. It

appeared that she was living with vagabonds. Gypsies,
as her grandmother had called them. Yes, that was it.
Gypsies. "Clay! Help me, please! Clay," she called,
weakly. "I need you. Where are you? Clay!" She
reached her arms for the illusive man of her dreams.

∞

Clay had read the list over and over so many times
that he was hoarse. He had only stopped long enough to
rest his voice. He was exhausted, so he lowered his head
on the bed next to Emmy's hand. He brushed his hair
because an irritating fly continued to land on him, and it
tickled. When he raised his head, he looked at her still
face. But what he saw excited him. Her eyes were
moving back and forth under her lids, almost in a panic,
and then he caught it. It had not been a fly brushing at
his hair. Her finger jumped.

"Nurse!"

Chapter Twenty-eight

The day Emmy's finger moved in a jerky spasm was exhilarating, but no one had seen it jump, since. Clay began to think he had been dreaming, because right before it happened, his head was resting on the bed. Maybe he had fallen asleep, and had transferred his dream into reality. The staff was kind. No one criticized him for his delusion. They said often a patient would have a muscle spasm and that could have been what he saw. Nothing more than a reflex from a body that was beginning to atrophy. That word frightened Clay. Now he feared that if she ever did wake up, she might not even be able to walk.

Clay was at home, having a late-night drink. Life was so lonely without Emmy. In the short time they had had, he had gotten used to having her in his life on a daily basis. They were a perfect match, and he had been excited to see what life had to offer them. But he was beginning to lose hope. Maybe Emmy would never come out of the coma, and she would waste away surrounded by strangers. He had to do something. Reading the list had produced some eye movement, and even though he continued to read it aloud, the staff at the rehab facility had no idea what he was doing. He always took a book with him, and when someone came in, he switched quickly to reading from those pages.

Clay had only run into Marge and Ken once. He was on his way out of Emmy's room when they were coming in. It had been awkward, but Ken had smiled at him, and asked how Emmy was doing that day. Marge had kept her head turned away, as if she was busy looking for something in her purse. Clay realized things would never be the same between them, but he didn't care. As long as he was allowed to see Emmy, he would continue to visit her. He was never going to give up on her.

Clay swirled his rum and coke around in the glass, letting the ice clink on the sides. Sitting in front of the fire, reminded him of that night Emmy had lost Tessie and they had gotten drenched in the rain. They had sat in front of this very fire, wrapped in towels. It was such a memorable night. Clay would never forget Emmy's wet hair hanging down her back, her trusting eyes, and her flawless skin. She was so lovely. He had thought she was married to Ken, but, even so, he had wanted her so badly. When Emmy learned about his mistake, she had laughed at him, but he didn't care because her giggles were the sound of angels. How he wished he could hear that laugh again. After clearing up the misconception, they shared their first kiss, and she had agreed to see him again. Clay sighed. It was almost torture to remember Emmy like that, but he could not stop. He needed to see her that way in his mind's eye. If he could will her back to life, he would, but nothing seemed to work.

Clay rose to look out at the dark sky. It was late; he couldn't see the lake any longer, and because of the clouds there were no stars showing in the sky. The days were dreary now, lots of rain which would soon turn to snow. It would be a long winter without her. Clay dreamed for the days of sunshine when he could take Emmy out on the boat and make passionate love to her again. Their first boat trip, when he had placed the bracelet on her wrist, was something he would cherish for the rest of his life. The bracelet had brought them together, he was sure of it now, the same way that the ruby necklace had worked for Ivy and Fox. Clay no longer questioned its magical powers. He believed the bracelet had been trying to put him with Emmy all along, but to what end? To watch her lie in a bed and waste away? He just didn't understand. The bracelet seemed like it was meant for life, joy, and happiness. It didn't make sense.

Clay stopped breathing for a moment. What a fool he had been! The bracelet! Of course. It was the answer. It must be. Clay's heart began to race, because he thought he knew how to reach Emmy. Maybe its power could pull her up from her deep sleep. The question was: how could he get away with it at the nursing home? And did he dare? Who knew what would happen if he placed it on her wrist? It produced electrical charges of some kind; they might be too strong. The intense desire it had brought to them the night on the boat might be too much for her. Clay could end up being the one responsible for her death. If that happened, how would he ever be able to live with himself? Did he dare to try?

Clay walked to the sink and dumped his drink. He ran upstairs and took the bracelet out of the safe. Small sparks jumped at his touch. He studied it carefully. The sapphires had been set in a wave-like pattern, and their deep blue had always reminded him of a river. Yes, it was clear to him now. He did dare. He had to do it. Tomorrow he would use this river's current to bring his love back. He smiled with excitement. Clay was sure sleep would not come to him tonight.

"Emmy," he whispered. "You're almost home. Hang on. I'm coming. Tomorrow, my sweet. I promise."

∞

Clay was up at six. He showered, had his coffee, and then he watched the clock, willing it to move to nine o'clock when visiting hours began. With the bracelet in his jacket pocket, he went out into the cold nippy morning to his car. He raised the garage door, and discovered a light dusting of frost. The grass was covered with diamonds, twinkling and beckoning him to proceed with his plan. He hopped in the car, backed around the turnaround, and drove out toward the street. But just before he reached the street, he glanced to his left, and he saw Ken and Marge exiting their driveway. His heart sank. They might not be going to the home, they could be going out for groceries or to breakfast, but he couldn't take a chance. He needed to be there all alone, with no risk of anyone showing up. He turned the car around and went back into the house. He paced back and forth, wondering how he would know when they returned. The only thing to do was to wait until after lunch. Clay had always been a patient man, but this morning the passing of time was torture.

Maria made him his favorite panini. He ate without tasting; he swallowed without thinking. He stared into nothingness. He only had one thing on his mind.

When his phone rang he jumped and almost decided not to answer it, but when he glanced at the screen and saw that it was Ivy, he picked up.

"Hello, Ivy. How are you?"

"I'm fine, Clay. The more important question is: how are you?"

"I'm good. I'm just wasting some time before I go to see Emmy."

"Any change?"

"Actually, there was one thing, but no one saw it but me. She raised a finger. They said it was a muscle reflex. Thing is, I don't believe them. I think she was trying to reach out to me."

"You might be right, but they are the professionals. I'm sure they've seen this happen many times before."

"Perhaps, but I can't give up hope. Did you just call to say hello? How is the little peanut coming along?"

Ivy laughed. "I've forgotten what a long wait it is until a baby is born. I'm ready now, but I still have a few months to go."

"When are you due again?"

"March 10th. It was my mother's birthday, so I hope the date is accurate."

"That would be special for you. Maybe she'll bring an early spring with her."

"I hope so. I'm dreading winter already. I've never been a fan. Listen, Clay, I didn't just call to see how Emmy was. I have some news."

"About Artem?"

"Yes, your birth father. I know you haven't paid much attention to your DNA test, so I'm glad you gave me the password to your account."

"You're right. I never gave it another thought after I came back from London. Once my mother had decided not to stay in touch with me, I gave up on that. And since Emmy's accident, I've totally forgotten about my birth father."

"Well, after some digging, I found your name down a ways on the list of connections with Fox. You are definitely on his line. Now we know it's just not the Karpenko name that matches his; you truly are family, according to the DNA test. I'm not sure where you fit, and of course there are no records of births for gypsies in Eastern Europe, but I believe that you might be off of the line of Beauregard Karpenko, also known as Bo in my book and his father Stas. If you recall, Bo and Anya were lovers and they were kept apart through various circumstances. Bo had an older brother, though, who was supposed to be king, but he died; therefore the royal roll passed on to Bo, which was why he could not marry Anya. I think *your* Karpenko line came from Bo's brother."

"It makes sense, doesn't it? I guess we'll never know for sure, will we? But at least with the DNA match, I know I am legitimately in Fox's family tree. That feels good. You are great people, and I have always felt blessed to know you."

"Thank you, Clay. We love having you in our family. And with Emmy's connection to Gina, it all falls into place. I'm sure it's the reason the bracelet works for you two."

Clay hesitated to say what he was thinking, but if he could share with anyone, it would be Ivy. "Ivy, I have a plan to reach Emmy, but I'm scared out of my wits to try it."

"What is it?"

Clay looked around to make sure Maria was not within hearing range. "I'm going to see her in a few minutes, and I'm going to place the bracelet on her wrist."

Ivy sucked in her breath. "Oh, my. Do you think that's safe?"

"I don't know. What do you think? It could bring her out of the coma, or it could kill her."

"I don't know what to tell you, I'm not a doctor, but I do know one thing. If it was Fox lying in that bed, I would use whatever means necessary to reach him."

"That's what I thought you would say. Thanks, you've helped me to make the decision to go ahead. I'm leaving shortly, so wish me luck," said Clay, shakily.

"I'll do more than that. I'll be praying for you, Clay."

"Thank you, Ivy. I appreciate that." Clay wiped a tear from the corner of his eye, said goodbye to his dear friend, then he grabbed his jacket, touched the sapphires in his pocket, and left.

Chapter Twenty-nine

Clay signed in at the front desk, and then went directly to Emmy's room. He had a difficult time not running through the halls. He was pleased to see that they were alone. He was so glad that she had a private room; the only ones who would bother her now, would be an occasional nurse coming in to check her monitors and feeding tube, et cetera. He could see that she had been bathed this morning. Her hair still a little damp, had been washed and braided; a long rope had been brought forward over her shoulder. With her hair like that, she looked even more exotic than ever before. He kissed her gently, stepped back to watch her face for eye movement, and then looked down at her hands. Nothing. He was hoping against hope that he would not have to take this drastic step. With his heart racing in his chest, he sat next to her, and began to read. He went through the list two times, and he noticed when he got to the last section, where he kept repeating Gina, he saw a tiny flicker of her eyelashes. He kissed her lips a little more forcefully and tried it again. This time he saw some rapid eye movement. It was obvious the name reading was reaching her, but just not enough to bring her out of it. Was it possible she liked where she was? Was her dream more enticing than reality?

Clay's shoulders were tense, his brow produced tiny droplets of water with an outward display of his nerves. He rotated his shoulders to ease the tension, then he slowly began to take out the bracelet. First, he placed it on the sheet next to her body. The small sparks began to shoot out. He glanced over his shoulder to make sure no one was in the hallway. When he heard a small moan from Emmy, he almost panicked. He was hoping nothing she did would set off alarms or monitors. He pulled the bracelet away from her again. Her eye movement continued, but she seemed less frantic than she had yesterday. It was working; he was sure of it.

∞

Gina was in a deep sleep. She loved sleeping. Her blankets wrapped her like a cocoon. Next to making love, sleeping was her favorite thing to do. Today's sleep was so comforting; she really needed the comfort, especially after Stas had told her that he was choosing Olnya as his queen. Snuggling down, she relished the warmth of her furs. The fresh straw bedding smelled so earthy. Sleep would help her unborn child to grow strong within her. She would need to stay healthy if she was to produce his first heir. But try as she might to stay in the safe place of dreams, she was slowly beginning to wake. She had been dreaming of Stas making love to her in all of their favorite places. She dreamed of them spending the day together at the river's edge, its waters slowly moving past them in blue undulating waves dusted with diamond sparkles which had reflected from the sun. In her dream, they threw tiny pebbles making splashes and ripples, and they watched as the passing water carried their love to distant places they had talked about visiting together someday. Gina moved a little and felt a body next to hers. She knew instantly that it was Stas. His scent was ingrained in her mind. He began caressing her naked skin under the covers, stroking her rounded belly where their child was growing. She moaned slightly and moved toward him, then as he hungrily kissed her, he quickly placed the bracelet on her wrist. He had come back to her, if only for a few moments, before returning to his future queen. This time, she didn't care what his reason was. She was eager for him. She would take him any way she could get him. The bracelet had shown on many occasion that she belonged to him. She would always belong to him. It was written in the stars. He whispered her name over and over, and she cried in his arms, as he said. "Gina, Gina, Gina."

∞

Clay slowly moved the bracelet again until it touched her fingers. The sparks were stronger, but they left no marks on the sheets or her flesh. Her eye movements became more erratic, so he cautiously moved the sapphires up toward her palm. When he saw no change in her monitors, he slipped it over her wrist. The sparks were wild now, shooting off in all directions. Clay held his breath, for what he was about to do next could change everything. He bent her arm at the elbow and placed her wrist over her heart, and all the while he chanted her ancestor name list, and when he got to the end where he was saying 'Gina, Gina, Gina,' she opened her eyes, looked at him with tears, then smiled with joy.

Her voice was soft and raspy, but he clearly heard her whisper, "Stas."

∞

Clay was shocked at hearing someone else' name coming from her lips, especially the name of a man who had been born in the 1820s. He had fantasized about how when she first saw him, she would throw her arms around his neck and call his name over and over. But another man had claimed that honor. At first, he didn't know how to handle the fact that she had taken him for someone else; someone born so long ago on another continent, someone she had never met. He did not have a clue how that was possible, but just the fact that she was awake was enough for him, now. Tears filled his eyes, and a stifled sob escaped, but when the monitors went off, sending sounds that echoed throughout the halls, and he could hear feet approaching, he quickly slipped the bracelet off and tucked it into his pocket.

Fear set in, as he saw Emmy's eyes close, then flutter open again a few times, and finally close for good. He was losing her, but he dared not take the bracelet out of his pocket. As the staff worked on her, and called her name, he stood anxiously next to the bed near her feet. It was the closest he could get to her. He thought the bracelet might be able to work through his pocket, but it looked as though she didn't have enough strength or will to come back to the surface of her dreams. She was giving up. She was slipping away.

In a panic, he pushed a nurse aside, leaned over her, and began calling her name.

"Emmy, come back to me. Emmy, can you hear me? Emmy, my darling, please, I need you."

The nurses who were present were overtaken with emotion at seeing Clay's desperation. They moved away from the bed and gave him room. He leaned over her, peppering her with kisses, and when he did his jacket pocket fell forward and touched her wrist. With his back to them, no one saw the sparks shooting through the fabric.

Clay stroked her hair and kissed her forehead, all the while calling her name. And with one last shower of sparks, she opened her eyes, and simply said, "Clay? Where am I?"

Everyone around the bed cheered silently, as they gave the thumbs-up gestures, not wanting to scare the patient.

Emmy tried to sit up, but found she was lightheaded. Even though enough time had passed for all of her wounds and breaks to heal, she had not used her muscles in months, and she was very weak.

One of the nurses said, "I'll go call the doctor and contact the relatives." And then she looked at Clay apologetically. She knew as soon as Marge and Ken arrived, things would change for him. He might even be pushed right out of the room, because he had no legal rights. The entire staff had fallen in love with Clay since Emmy had been there. He was always polite and respectful, but beside that, he was tall, drop-dead gorgeous, and his British accent made all of the ladies swoon. Whenever he was in the room, some of the nurses would make excuses to see how Emmy was doing, just to get a better look at him. On the way out the door, the nurse who was going to contact Marge, whispered, "Sorry," and patted his arm.

Once Emmy's vitals were checked and she was comfortable, everyone left the room, so the two lovers could have some alone time together. Clay could not stop looking at Emmy. She was back, his Emmy had come back to him. He didn't even care why she had called him Stas. He knew mysterious forces had been at work when he placed the sapphires on her arm, but he would think about that later. For now it was enough that she was awake and alert.

"What happened, Clay?" Emmy asked after having a few sips of water. "Why am I here? And where is 'here' exactly?"

Clay didn't know how much he should tell her, so he kept it simple. "You were in a car accident, and you broke several bones and had a lot of cuts and bruises. But don't worry, my sweet, you're all healed now."

"Healed? How can I be all healed? How long have I been here? I don't remember anything, except..."

Clay saw the look on her face. She became quite pale as her thoughts traveled back to the gypsy camp. "Stas," she longingly whispered. Then she looked at

Clay, and said, "I was at a – no, it can't be. But it was all so real." She put her hand on her abdomen, and asked, "Am I pregnant?"

"Pregnant? No, sweets, you are not pregnant."

Then she said the strangest thing, "My baby, my baby girl, Gina." And tears flowed from her eyes. "She never had a fair life, because I was not able to make Stas love me enough. I was meant to marry the king, but Olnya married him instead. Later, she had two sons and one was named Bo. The rubies are stronger than the sapphires. She won." Then Emmy cried as though she had just experienced a great loss.

Clay wrapped her in his arms, and rocked her like a baby. He caressed her hair and wiped her tears. "It's all in the past, Emmy. It happened so very long ago. I'm here. And if you'll have me, we can put things right. I have so much to tell you. I love you with all of my heart, my sweets. Besides, the sapphires have plenty of strength for us. It's all we'll ever need, as long as we have each other."

Emmy sobbed in his arms. "But I am lost without them. I feel so empty. My child. My baby." But when she lifted her head and looked into Clay's eyes, she was pulled back into reality once again. This was the man she truly loved, and the one who loved her in return. The bracelet was trapped between them, and her heart swelled with passion. "Clay, oh my, Clay. I have missed you so."

When Clay stared deeply into her beautiful eyes, he saw that his Emmy was back. All signs of Gina were gone. He felt a stirring of desire, and as soon as he was able to clear his head, he removed his jacket and placed it on a chair far away from them. He was terrified that once the sapphires were no longer in contact with her skin, she would leave him again, but it did not happen this time. It seemed that she was back for good, and he would see to it that that is where she remained.

In the middle of one of their kisses, Marge cleared her throat, having quietly entered the room. Ken was standing right behind her. She looked tearful, but excited. And as she glanced at Clay, for the first time since his blowup at their house, he saw remorse. She went to Emmy and hugged her, and welcomed her back. Then she turned to Clay, and said quietly, "Forgive me, please?"

He gave a short nod, just enough so that Marge knew he was willing to put the past behind him, but not enough for Emmy to see their exchange. She smiled and Ken clapped him on the back.

The doctor came in and gave Emmy a complete examination. He said she was in perfect health and could go home in a day or two. They just wanted to make sure she was completely hydrated, all of her organs were functioning properly, and she could tolerate normal food again.

When he left, Clay turned to the Thompsons, and said, "I know that I am not a relative and have no rights, but I would love to take Emmy home with me. I can hire a full-time nurse, and I'll pay for a physical therapist to come to the house daily. She will be well-cared for. I intend to marry Emmy, if she'll have me, so you'd better get used to me being in the family."

Marge nodded, then looked at Ken for approval. Always a quiet man, words were not that important to him, he simply shook Clay's hand and said, "Anything you want, Clay."

Ken was surprised Marge had caved in so easily. She always seemed to be looking for a fight, but what he did not know was that Marge had recently gotten wind of Clay's wealth, which as she surmised was even more vast than Ken's. Her little sister had hit the jackpot, and she fully intended to ride on Emmy's coattails.

∞

Just as the doctor had promised, two days later, Emmy was curled up on Clay's couch, with a comfortable pillow at her head and a warm blanket over her legs. Maria loved having her there, and couldn't get enough of pampering her. Emmy was alert and almost back to normal, except for some weakness in her legs. Her recovery had been absolutely remarkable.

Clay was surprised when one day, she said, "We need to talk. I have to tell you an amazing tale. It's a story of a gypsy girl and a handsome gypsy prince, who looked exactly like you."

Chapter Thirty

Several weeks later, after intense physical therapy, Emmy was completely back to normal. Her workouts had been grueling at times, but she had done everything she was supposed to, from learning how to handle stairs, to grasping and picking up kitchen items. If the weather had been better, Emmy and Clay would have taken walks around the lake or at least up and down the driveway, but winter was moving in early. There was already a light dusting of snow on the ground and bitter winds were blowing off of Muskegon Lake, pushed from behind by the blasts coming off of Lake Michigan.

The two lovers spent a lot of time by the fire, reading and talking in low tones about everything from 'soup to nuts' as Emmy liked to say. They never ran out of topics of conversation. But one particular topic had been avoided since Emmy had told Clay about her time in the gypsy camp in her dream. Clay was actually afraid to go there. He was worried that she might want to return. He wasn't sure if a person could will themselves back into a coma or not, but he did not want to find out. Finally, one night when the fire was especially cozy and the classical music of Mozart had lulled them into a comfortable zone, Emmy decided the time was right to discuss what was on her mind.

"Clay."

"Hmm?" he said softly, as he nibbled her neck.

"We need to talk."

"Haven't we talked enough for one night? Aren't you ready for another type of recreation?"

Emmy laughed. Clay always seemed to have one thing on his mind. It was not that she objected, she was more than willing to be an eager participant, but she had decided she had to get some things off of her mind. She gently pushed him away.

"Sit there, a little away from me, please."

"Yes, madam. Anything you wish. What's so important that I have to interrupt my very important work?"

"First of all, I want to say thank you for all you did for me while I was in the hospital. I know it wasn't easy."

"It was not, I'll grant you that, but I would not want to be anywhere else, as long as you were ill. I'll always be there for you, sweetheart; I hope you know that."

"I do now. And I trust you completely, but I need to explain why I left you."

"I'd rather forget about it, if you don't mind," said Clay, looking down at his hands.

"No, I have to tell you. Please listen."

"Okay, I'll keep an open mind. Go ahead."

"You know about my visions. I told you about them when we were on the boat."

"Yes, I remember."

"Well, what I didn't tell you is that I knew how I was going to die. I saw it, and it terrified me."

"You saw it? That's horrible. I can't imagine anything worse."

"The thing is I saw myself in a terrible car accident, rolling over and over. I knew you wanted to go on a road trip to St. Ignace, and I was afraid if you and I were in a car together that you would die, too, so I left. I left to protect you, not because I didn't love you."

"But you were wrong. You didn't die."

"Here's the thing, Clay. My vision didn't have a timestamp. Maybe that was the accident I saw, and I pulled through anyway, because of you. Or maybe I am still going to be in another accident that will kill me. It might not have happened yet. I'm not sure I want to risk you being around me when that happens."

"Emmy, Emmy, my darling. There are no guarantees in life. We all have to go sometime, and if we go together, then that's fine with me. I plan on being with you until the end of time, if you'll have me."

"Oh Clay, how have I lived this long without you? You are my life."

"And mine too, sweets. Let's make a pact not to talk about our deaths ever again. When it happens it happens. Okay?"

"Okay, yes, but there is something else. I know we only talked once about what happened while I was in my coma, and it was pretty general. I think we need to go into it a little deeper."

"Why? I understand it was all a dream. It meant nothing. You were confused."

"But was it just a dream, Clay? Was I confused? It seemed way more than that to me."

"The doctor said they have no idea what goes through a person's mind while they are in a coma. I asked when it first happened to you. He said most times when people come out of the coma they remember nothing. It's like no time had passed. He also said there was a possibility you could hear me talking, as I read your grandmother's list over and over to try to reach you.

You might have heard me saying Gina, and it triggered something in your imagination"

"But that's just it. This was not like a regular dream. I was really there!"

"I know it must seem that way, but how could it be. Your body was always in the bed, so logically, it's impossible. What you were talking about, if it really happened, took place over 200 years ago. Can't you see that it was all a dream? Gina is not real, and Stas is not real, and of course you were not pregnant."

"But Clay, you know, and I know, and Ivy and Fox know, that Gina and Stas *are* real – or were in their own time. Ivy knew about a Gina from her research, who was in Bo and Anya's story. I've been thinking about this a lot. Their Gina was my Gina's daughter. She was the baby that Gina was carrying."

Clay knew it all sounded like nonsense, but who was he to discount fantasy and mystical happenings. He believed in the bracelet, he had seen for himself how it worked, and he had met someone named Gina himself in London. She may also have been the old woman in the parking lot. Emmy watched Clay's face as he began to sort out facts he had not wanted to visit before.

"Strange as it sounds, I think you're right. *Ivy's* Gina is the same one who disrupted plans for Bo and Anya to be together. *Your* Gina was her mother, and because *that* Gina got pregnant with Stas' child, she disrupted a chain of events that were meant to happen, also. Who knows if Olnya or Gina was the right match for Stas, but he obviously loved them both. Then Bo, Stas' son, and the next Gina might have finally gotten together, but he fell in love with Anya, the Ukrainian peasant girl, and according to Ivy's book, the ruby necklace brought them together until Gina tore them apart again."

"Yes," agreed Emmy, "and look at how she appeared to you in London. She was trying once more to put things right. She recognized who you were and knew that you needed to find me. I am her descendant."

"And I am Stas's descendant." As soon as it was said aloud, Clay realized what Gina had meant in the

London fortunetelling shop. *"She belongs to me, and therefore I belong to you."*

"What do you mean? I don't get it." She could see that Clay was getting excited with his new revelation.

"That's what Gina told me in England. Those were her exact words. They were etched in my brain, and they were always very confusing to me. I was hoping for some clarity, so I asked the investigator I had hired to find my mother, to stop by the shop where I got the bracelet. I requested that he ask Gina to clear that phrase up, but when he got to the address I had given him, everything was gone. All signs of the shop had disappeared. Poof, like magic." Clay's face lit up with excitement. "Don't you see what she was saying? It all makes sense now."

Emmy leaned forward. "Explain, please."

"*She belongs to me*, means you, of course. You are the child of *her* child's descendants. I guess I knew that part, but the other part eluded me until just now. *I belong to you* means that she, Gina, belongs to *me*, because I am a descendant of Stas. And she always believed she belonged to him."

"I think you're right, Clay. Our family tree is so entangled, but aren't they all. I always wondered if some people that are a couple today had relatives that were together in a past life. Because of all of Ivy's research, the Gina encounters, the jewels, and my grandmother's list, we now know it's true. It can happen, and does. We were meant to be together. It was destiny."

"You are my Gina," said Clay softly, as he slid closer to her. "My Emmaline Regina Simmons. Shall I call you Gina from now on?"

"Please don't," laughed Emmy. "Emmy will do just fine."

Then Clay slid off of the couch and got down on one knee. He took Emmy's hands in his, and said, "Well, then, Emmy Simmons, since we were meant to be together from the beginning of time, will you do me the honor of becoming my wife?"

Emmy had not been expecting a proposal so soon, she had thought there would be more of a courtship, but they had lost so much time already, and life was short.

So she joyfully said without hesitation, "Yes. I will be your wife. Yes. Yes. Yes."

Beaming from ear to ear, Clay explained, "I had planned a proper proposal, but I couldn't contain myself any longer. I don't have an engagement ring yet -- well, I do, but I'm having a one-of-kind custom ring made especially for you. Will this do for now?" And he slid the sapphire bracelet out of his pocket and moved it onto her wrist.

"Mr. Harris, I would be proud to wear this bracelet for you. Just don't ask me to wear it in public." And with that the two lovers wrapped their arms around each other and fell to the floor, their love and desire for one another heightened by sapphires and diamonds. All around them, flying sparks put on a splendorous show, declaring this union to be finalized at last. If someone had been walking by the plate glass window that looked out onto the lake, they would have seen an indoor firework display, shooting out all the colors of the rainbow.

∞

On the other side of the ocean, in a little mystical shop in London, an exotic woman with long dark hair named Gina, danced around and around holding a swirl of colorful scarves above her head, while bangles clinked together on her arms and ropes of beads moved over her breasts. She played the tambourine, tapping her fingers on the skin, keeping time to the rhythm of her culture and the music of her ancestors. Swaying to the steady beat, she smiled happily while singing an ancient Romani song in her native tongue; then she chanted the words which belonged to a melody she knew so well. "She belongs to me, and therefore I belong to you. I belong to you. I belong to you."

∞

Author's Notes

Spoiler Alert!!

When I began writing this series, it was meant to be a standalone book called Ruby and Sal, but about three quarters of the way in, I knew it had to be more. The story of the ruby and diamond necklace had to be told, so I forged ahead with Maisy and Max, and Ivy and Fox, thinking I had reached a conclusion. But as sometimes happens the characters dictate the story, not the author. I didn't think my readers would be satisfied unless I found Fox's son, and so book 4, Georgy and Jack, came into being. Michael was meant to be a minor player, to confuse the reader and question which one of the men was Fox's son, but as time went on I could see he had a story to tell, also. Little did I know that would mean another piece of jewelry would appear in my story, until one day I was digging around in my jewelry box, looking for something to go with my outfit, when I came upon a bracelet that I had had for over thirty years.

There was a time in my life when my husband and I owned antique shops. And as is often the case, when you have an actual storefront, people bring you things they want to sell. One particular woman brought in many pieces of jewelry that had belonged to her mother-in-law who had recently passed away. Her mother-in-law was of Italian descent and had immigrated right after World War II as a war bride. She brought with her about fifteen sets of earrings, all the screw-on type of the era, and a beautiful bracelet. The strange thing about these pieces is that every one of them was synthetic sapphire and cubic zirconia. Apparently, the mother-in-law only wore blue sapphire jewelry because she had dark hair and very blue eyes. It was all she had in her jewelry box at the time of her death. I ended up buying all of it from her, I don't have a clue why, because I knew the earrings would be difficult to sell because of the screw backs. I was very attracted to the bracelet for some reason, and actually hoped it wouldn't sell. Eventually, I sold all of the earrings but the bracelet remained, until one day I took it home with me. I took it out and handled it on occasion, but it seemed a little gaudy at the time, so I only wore it once or twice when I was going to a formal party, then I put it away in my jewelry box and there it sat for twenty-eight years. I would take it out and handle it once in a while. I liked the feel of it in my hands. It was flexible and cool and sparkled in the light. This time as I held it, it suddenly became clear that it was another piece that could be used in my story. When I showed it to my husband and told him my idea, he suggested we take it to a jewelry store and see what they had to say about it, which we did. We were right. It was synthetic sapphires and CZs. And just as we suspected all along, it had some value, but it was not the 'real deal.' The clerk was curious about it also, so she said she would like to clean it. She did a fabulous job on it, and when she brought it back out to me, I could not believe my eyes. It had truly transformed into the bracelet I had imagined it to be in Emmy and Clay. Don't ask. It does not have any magical properties. I'm still waiting for Gina to appear someday, but so far -- nothing. I'll keep a look out for her and let you know; maybe there's another piece of jewelry yet to be discovered, but as far as I know this is the end of the series. If you have any fantastic ideas, please let me know. I hope you enjoyed The Unforgettables as much as I enjoyed writing it.

Don't forget to leave a review or comment when you finish reading. I read every one, and they are always so appreciated.

To find more of my books, go to my author page at Amazon:

https://www.amazon.com/Jane-OBrien/e/B00XRPNCG4

Follow me on Goodreads:

https://www.goodreads.com/author/show/8064
64.Jane_O_Brien

Follow me on Facebook:

https://www.facebook.com/janeobrien.author/

Follow me on Twitter:

https://twitter.com/janeobrienbooks

Follow me on Instagram:

https://www.instagram.com/author_jane_obrien

∞

Bibliography

Father Jacques Marquette is the subject of Clay's research, and therefore also became the subject of mine. We learned a little bit about him in school, but I had long since forgotten most of it, so I had to dig into various

Internet sites and books to find out everything I would need to know to write my story.

He was truly a very interesting man and an American hero, and if you would like to look further into his life, here are some of the links I used to study him. And if you live in Michigan or if you are ever visiting Michigan, take some time to visit his final resting place in St. Ignace at the Father Marquette National Memorial or stop by the memorial cross in Ludington, as Emmy and Clay did.

Father Marquette: Illustrated, by Reuben Gold Thwaites

https://www.nps.gov/nr/travel/cultural_diversity/father_marquette_national_memorial.html

https://en.wikipedia.org/wiki/Jacques_Marquette

https://en.wikipedia.org/wiki/Pere_Marquette_Beach

https://www.facebook.com/pages/Father-Marquette-Memorial-Cross/139056382798017

Made in the USA
Monee, IL
02 December 2020